THE TUNNEL
TO YESTERDAY

Other Avon Camelot Books by
Jerome Beatty, Jr.

JEROME BEATTY, JR., has written many books for young readers. A former newspaper and magazine editor, his articles have appeared in many publications. Born in New York, Mr. Beatty was graduated from Dartmouth College. He now lives on Cape Cod with his family.

ERIC JON NONES was born in Pennsylvania. He received a degree in Fine Arts from Rutgers University and an Associate Degree in illustration from Pratt. He lives in New York City.

THE TUNNEL TO YESTERDAY

Jerome Beatty, Jr.

Illustrated by Eric Jon Nones

AN AVON CAMELOT BOOK

UNNEL TO YESTERDAY is an original publication of
Books. This work has never before appeared in book
.

grade reading level has been determined by using the Fry
Readability Scale.

AVON BOOKS
A division of
The Hearst Corporation
959 Eighth Avenue
New York, New York 10019

Library of Congress Cataloging in Publication Data

Beatty, Jerome.
   The tunnel to yesterday.

   (An Avon/Camelot book)
   Summary: Amateur archaeologist Sam Churchill,
hired by a Mayflower descendant to help clear her
family name from an ancient plot, travels through a
time tunnel to seventeenth-century Plymouth.
   [1. Mystery and detective stories. 2. Archaeology
— Fiction. 3. Space and time—Fiction. 4. Pilgrims
(New Plymouth Colony)—Fiction] I. Title.
PZ7.B380542Tu   1983   [Fic]   82-90557
ISBN 0-380-82537-6

First Camelot Printing, March, 1983

To Judy and Eddie

TABLE OF CONTENTS

1. TINKERTON MANOR

THE BUS slowed down as it passed a red, white and blue sign.

WELCOME TO PLYMOUTH
AMERICA'S HOME TOWN

Sam Churchill sat up and began getting his things together. A paper bag with a soft banana in it, all that was left of the lunch his mother had given him when he left Junction City, Kansas, twenty-four hours earlier. An empty thermos. A small bag holding odds and ends such as a toothbrush and toothpaste, with which he was supposed to have cleaned up at one of the rest stops. But he hadn't done it and now his teeth felt as though they were wearing little mittens.

The bus turned in to the main street, went a few blocks in heavy traffic and pulled into the terminal.

"This is it, folks," the driver announced. Passengers straggled out to wait for their baggage to be unloaded.

9

Sam picked up his suitcase and looked around. He had done his part, arriving on time. Now she had to do hers and pick him out in this mob of tourists. All she had to go on was the photograph he had sent along when he applied for the job, answering an ad in *Junior Archeologist* magazine:

WANTED: *Circumspect, ambitious, historically minded young person to dig unexplored ruins. Low-paying, high-interest summer job working for* Mayflower *descendant. Must have curiosity and strong back. Send resume, references and photograph to Tinkerton Manor, Plymouth, Massachusetts.*

First he had looked up the meaning of circumspect. "Heedful of consequences; prudent."

"It just means keep your mouth shut," his father explained, "and don't go around blabbing about what you're doing."

Sam liked that. There was a feeling of mystery. "And I'm ambitious, and I like history," he added.

"He has curiosity, all right," his mother said, smiling at Mr. Churchill and remembering how Sam had always wanted to know the why's and wherefore's of everything. Once, as a little boy, he had emptied the refrigerator, planning to climb in and shut the door to see if the light really went off. When he was older, he had made a pair of wings out of canvas and jumped off the barn roof in an attempt to fly. Luckily, he landed in a hay pile. One year he had spent a lot of time watching caterpillars, hoping to see one turn into a butterfly.

Now he was high on archeology, and he had dug many holes in the backyard, unearthing a lot of old bottles and cans. On a trip to an ancient Indian burial mound on the banks of the Smoky Hill River, he had discovered a pair of red suspenders that were now on exhibit in a glass case in the Junction City library.

His parents had let him answer the advertisement because they never for a moment thought he would get the job. But they were wrong. Back came a letter from a Miss Elvira Tinkerton, the *Mayflower* descendant, asking a lot of questions. She was satisfied with his answers, and was especially pleased when she learned that an ancestor of his, too, had arrived in the New World at around the time of the Pilgrims. She hired him.

It was too late for Sam's parents to say no and so they had agreed to let their boy go off to a strange town for the summer. They gave him advice, warnings, fifteen dollars and a new no-wind battery wristwatch. They put him on a bus to Boston, where he changed for the local to Plymouth.

And here he was. But where was Miss Tinkerton? He was startled to hear, "Master Samuel, I presume?" He turned to find a distinguished-looking gentleman who wore black shoes, black trousers, white shirt and a black bow tie.

"That's me," Sam replied. "I mean, I am him— he—or that is I. Take your choice."

"Good." The man picked up the suitcase. "I am Diggins, Miss Tinkerton's factotum. Please follow me."

"Fack-what-um?" Sam asked. But the fellow was already threading his way through the crowd, headed toward the parking lot. Sam hurried after him. When Diggins opened the rear door of a shiny silver Rolls Royce for him, Sam climbed in, pretending that he was an old Rolls rider. He settled down on the nice upholstery and a minute later they were gliding smoothly south on the main street, Diggins at the wheel. It sure was a lot more comfortable than the bus. So this was the town founded by the Pilgrims! Pretty exciting for a lad from the Midwest who had never been so far away from home before.

"By the way, Diggins," he said, "where is the Rock?"

But Diggins didn't reply. Sam was thinking that was quite impolite when he realized there was a pane of glass between the driver's seat and himself. Diggins hadn't heard the question. Sam was about ready to shout when he noticed a telephone at his elbow. He picked it up, pressed a button and saw Diggins lift a phone to his mouth.

"Yes, Master Samuel?"

"I was wondering where Plymouth Rock is."

Diggins tilted his head to indicate the direction. "We passed it. It's down another street. But we haven't time to stop there now, Master Samuel. Miss Tinkerton is expecting us momentarily."

"Why didn't she meet me at the bus station?"

"Miss Tinkerton seldom appears downtown."

"Why is that?"

"I am not at liberty to divulge that information,

12

Master Samuel. Perhaps Miss Tinkerton herself will feel free to do so."

Sam thanked him and hung up. Diggins went back to driving with two hands while the puzzled boy thought about what he had just been told. Wow, imagine a descendant of the first Pilgrims who stayed away from the great historical places that were such a big part of her past! Maybe there was a mystery here after all. And if she told him about it, he would remember to be *circumspect*.

A few minutes later the car reached the edge of town, turned through a gate and went up a long, winding driveway. This was Tinkerton Manor according to the wrought-iron letters over the gateway. When the main house finally came into sight, Sam saw that it was a mansion, with towers, high windows and several chimneys. It was surrounded by gardens, a lawn and a forest that seemed to stretch without end. As the limousine circled the driveway and came to a stop, the front door opened and a woman stepped onto the verandah. Diggins came around the car and let his passenger out.

"Ah, Samuel," the woman called in friendly greeting. "Welcome. I am Miss Tinkerton."

Sam climbed the steps and shook her hand. She seemed to be about the same age as his mother although she was much thinner. Her eyeglasses hung around her neck by a string. Her hair was tied up in a big bun and her dress went clear down to her ankles, where a pair of high-button shoes could be seen.

"How do you do," he said politely.

She stepped back. "Let me look at you." What she saw was a sturdy young fellow with brown hair and blue eyes. What she didn't see, but would note later, was a bright kid with the curiosity she wanted for the job ahead. Also, he had a sense of humor that she would like. Sometimes it got him into trouble, like the time he had half the town out looking for a flying saucer.

She quickly made him feel at home. Diggins led the way to a room on the second floor. It was big and sunny, with a large Oriental rug, a feather mattress on a double bed and a private bath with a big old-fashioned tub. Diggins placed the suitcase on top of a chest and went out.

"Do you like it?" Miss Tinkerton asked.

Sam looked around. It was terrific. Through the big bay window he could see clear across a sunken garden to the meadows and the forest. "Do you own all this?" he asked.

"Acres and acres. Even the Indian mound where you will work."

"Where is it? I don't see it."

"It's through the woods, down by the water. It's too late now but in a day or two we'll go exploring, along with our expedition leader, Professor Pittfall."

"Not *the* Professor Pittfall?"

"Yes, the very one."

"Gee." Even young Sam had heard of Potter B. Pittfall, world-famous archeologist.

"I told you in one of my letters that this is a very serious project. That's why I have engaged him—at

14

great expense. He has given up his Egyptian tomb dig for the summer. You are to be his assistant. I am expecting great things from both of you. And at the same time, you will be learning from the best teacher there is."

"Boy, you can say that again!" Sam exclaimed.

Miss Tinkerton smiled and went to the door. "Now get yourself settled and then come on downstairs. We'll call your parents to tell them you've arrived safely and then you and I'll have a nice chat."

Diggins served tea and crumpets in the parlor while logs blazed in the fireplace. Sam had to answer Miss Tinkerton's questions about himself and his family before they began to talk about the summer project. He learned that the Indian mound was called Queppish Hill. Over the years no one had paid much attention to it because it was hidden away on Tinkerton private property, and also because historians had been more interested in the Rock, the *Mayflower* and other glamorous tourist attractions in downtown Plymouth.

"When I was a girl," Sam's hostess said, "I used to climb the hill just for fun. I had heard that it had some connection with our early family history but I didn't know what it was and I didn't care then. When I grew up and began to ask, I was told to forget about it."

"But now you're serious about digging into the mound?"

She put down her teacup and looked Sam in the

eye. "Yes, I am. It is the only place on the estate that hasn't been explored. Because I am the last Tinkerton, it has to be done now. Perhaps there is evidence inside Queppish Hill that will clear the Tinkerton name so that I shall be free to walk downtown with my head held high."

There was silence while Sam let that sink in. Miss Tinkerton's face was very grim, making him hesitate to ask the next question. Finally he decided to go ahead. He just had to know more.

"And why," he began carefully, "can't you—"

"That's enough," she interrupted. She blinked her eyes, shook her head and sighed deeply. "It's something we Tinkertons don't like to talk about." Then she smiled. "Now, come on, Sam, tell me more about your family. More tea?"

Later, when Sam climbed into his comfortable bed, he wondered about the rest of the story, hoping she would tell it all when Professor Pittfall arrived the next day.

The window was open and he heard the sounds of the night—peepers, a hoot owl, a distant motor car. When he turned out the light, the darkness jumped into the room with him. What was the mystery of Queppish Hill? He pulled the comforter up to his chin and, plenty tired, he fell asleep.

2. QUEPPISH HILL

AT BREAKFAST Diggins served scrambled eggs and bacon on a silver platter. After Miss Tinkerton made the toast, she opened a notebook and began to give Sam instructions about his new job.

"I can tell from talking to you that your studies of Plymouth have been rather weak. I am surprised, considering your connection with the colony through that ancestor of yours who is supposed to have been here at the the time the settlement was founded. Therefore, this morning you will start catching up by reading some books I have laid out for you in the library. Tomorrow you will go downtown, walk around and fill up on all the history you can. Visit the *Mayflower,* the old houses, the Rock, the museum, the ancient graves on Burial Hill, the Tunnel to Yesterday, the Plymouth Plantation, and, of course, the memorial to the Pilgrim women."

"What did they do?"

"What didn't they do! They worked and suffered. They sewed, laundered, cooked, gardened, raised babies. If a man fell sick, they put him to bed and cared for him. If a woman fell sick, she just kept on working."

Sam nodded. "That sounds like something my mother would say."

"Before you turn one shovelful of earth on Queppish Hill, I want you to know the whole story of the Plymouth colony. That goes for Professor Pittfall too."

"He probably already knows it."

"We shall see."

Following orders, Sam spent the morning in the Tinkerton library, reading through chapters of old books and rare papers that she had marked for him. He found nothing about his Churchill ancestor but he did learn a lot about the beginning of the colony.

Before the Pilgrims arrived, some sea captains had already explored the new land and named it New England. The *Mayflower* had really been headed for Virginia but had lost its course. Since the Pilgrims liked Cape Cod and Massachusetts when they landed, they decided to settle where they were.

The Indians had been friendly to them.

Some of the Pilgrims had stayed on the ship during the first winter while their houses were being built. Homes were finished for the families of Bradford, Hopkins, Tinkerton —

Sam perked up. This was getting interesting. Maybe he could solve the mystery by himself. But when he read on, he found no more about the family except that there were three Tinkertons aboard: the husband, his wife and one son. The father must have been an important fellow if one of the houses was being built for him. What went wrong?

Sam was still looking for an answer an hour later when the library door was thrown open and Miss Tinkerton stuck her head in. "Professor Pittfall is here!"

Sam followed her outside, where a safari wagon had stopped at the front door. The back seat was jammed with boxes, cases, instruments, tools and a jumble of gear. In the front seat was a big man who climbed out with a grin.

"My dear Miss Tinkerton, we meet again."

"Hello, Professor. I'm so glad you have arrived."

She introduced Sam, whose hand was almost lost in the fellow's grip.

"So you'll be my assistant," the great explorer and archeologist said. "You look sturdy enough and they tell me you're a smart one too."

"I'll try my best, sir."

Professor Pittfall was the largest—the fattest—man Sam had ever seen. He wore a topi (sun helmet), knee-length shorts of khaki, white cotton socks and desert boots. In the big accordionlike pockets of his bush jacket he had stuffed odds and ends, including a pipe and tobacco. One ear was decorated with a gold earring and under his nose he sported an enormous walrus mustache. After looking Sam over for a moment, he declared, "You're hired, young man. Now let's get started. How about lunch?"

19

That was when Sam first began to notice that food was just as important to the big fellow as archeology. Diggins carried a couple of the professor's bags up to his suite, where he took only a few minutes to wash up before coming back downstairs in search of the dining room.

Once he had swallowed about a quart of cold root beer and several ham and cheese sandwiches on rye bread, the professor relaxed and began to talk. Sam listened in awe to his interesting conversation. Potter B. Pittfall was known throughout the world. He had excavated ruins as far away as Mesopotamia and as nearby as Mississippi, where he had astounded men of science with his discovery of the wing bones of a flying dinosaur. His articles and books about his adventures and discoveries had been published in many countries. His latest book, *Dig, Man, Dig!*, was a best-seller.

"Yes, this job is going to be a real challenge," he boomed as he dug into a banana split that Diggins had prepared at his request. "Now, Miss Tinkerton, you must tell me all there is to know about this mysterious mound."

"That will have to wait until we visit it," she replied. "In the meantime, Professor, please call me Elvira."

He finished the banana split, giving a final lick to the spoon. "And you, my dear, may call me Potter."

Then, stuffing a handful of macaroons into a pocket, he stood up. "Now, let's have a look at your Queppish Hill, shall we?"

Soon Sam, the professor and Miss Tinkerton were

in the safari wagon, jouncing along a dirt road that led from the rear of the mansion into the woods. Miss Tinkerton, who had changed into slacks, sat in the front seat beside the professor. Sam perched in the rear on top of the equipment. Some of it he recognized, such as spades, shovels, hatchet, picks, hand trowels, brooms and small brushes. There were also many scientific instruments that meant nothing to him but he knew they must be important.

Following directions, the professor drove across the pasture, into the woods and along a pine-covered path just wide enough for the vehicle. They went down a slope and came to a body of water, where the path ended.

"Tinkerton Sea," Miss Tinkerton announced. "Salt water, connected to the ocean. From here we walk."

"Walk?" the archeologist echoed. "Potter B. Pittfall never walks." He patted the dashboard. "Old Lulu has taken me to the top of Mount Kilimanjaro and into Death Valley. She can surely carry us to Queppish Hill. Which way, Elvira?"

"Well, all right. To the left, along the shore."

"Forward, Lulu!" He stepped on the gas and swung the wheel. The wagon crashed through the underbrush while the passengers hung on. After what seemed a long time, they broke through a screen of cattails and into a clearing.

"Stop!" Miss Tinkerton cried, pointing straight ahead. "There it is!"

Queppish Hill did not look like much of a hill to

Sam. It was just a great big mound about two stories high, covered with small shrubs and weeds. But if Miss Tinkerton was right, inside were valuable secrets.

They all climbed out of the safari wagon. The professor pulled a camp chair out of the back, unfolded it and set it on the ground facing the hill. With a sigh, he lowered his huge bulk into the seat. After staring at the mound for some time in silence, he declared, "Very interesting. All right, let's get started." Rummaging in his pockets, he brought out notebook, pen, pipe and tobacco, and a steel tape measure. Handing the tape to Sam, he said, "I want to know the dimensions of this mound. Elvira, if you will be so kind."

She had just finished tacking onto a tree trunk the digging and camping permit Diggins had picked up at the town hall. She hurried over and held the end of the tape as Sam unwound it. Professor Pittfall puffed on his pipe and wrote down the figures they called out to him as they measured Queppish Hill. Every bush, tree and landmark was noted.

Finally the professor said, "All right, Sam, to the summit like a good fellow. Take a shovel."

Sam scrambled up the steep slope, something the archeologist would never be able to do.

"Are there any markings up there that might indicate an entrance?"

Sam went back and forth, scraping and poking the shovel into the ground. "No, sir."

When the survey was finished, they had a detailed

23

sketch of the hill and its surroundings. Sam was not surprised when Pittfall looked at his watch and announced, "Tea time!"

Miss Tinkerton was prepared. She spread a cloth over the pine needles and put out the cups and plates that Diggins had supplied. Tea was poured from a thermos bottle and watercress sandwiches and scones were served. Sam enjoyed the break. So far he felt pretty good about his summer job.

The professor finished his share of the food, lit his pipe again and relaxed. He hadn't moved from the chair yet. Miss Tinkerton packed up the picnic basket and said that she was going on an exploratory stroll in the woods. She put the compass in her pocket.

"Now let's set up camp," Professor Pittfall told Sam.

Having had experience at this, Sam had no trouble in finding a good spot and pitching the tent. He even made drainage ditches around the sides. The professor's chair was placed under the open front flap of the tent and the explorer sat there facing the mound. As soon as all the supplies had been stored inside, he said, "Now, Sam, we must have a latrine."

Sam picked up the shovel again, wondering about the man's use of the words "us" and "we." So far the professor had stood up only once, when his chair had been moved. But this is what I'm being paid for, Sam told himself. He went out into the woods about a hundred feet and dug a slit trench as he had been taught to do on camping trips.

Miss Tinkerton returned to report that she had circled the area and found nothing unusual. Professor Pittfall squinted across the water at the afternoon sun. "We had better start back now or we'll be late for dinner. When we return, we shall begin digging into the past."

With the stem of his pipe he pointed to a spot at the base of Queppish Hill. "Right there!"

3. PLYMOUTH

BUT BEFORE the digging began, Sam and Professor Pittfall spent a day in town. Sam went to catch up on his Pilgrim history, as Miss Tinkerton insisted he do. The professor, munching on a macaroon left in one of his pockets, said, "I just want to get the feel of the place."

They drove to Plymouth in the safari wagon. Their first stop was at the replica of the *Mayflower*, tied up at the wharf. It took only a few minutes to tour the tiny ship.

"Can you imagine being cooped up in here with a hundred other passengers for two months while you crossed the ocean?" the professor asked.

"No, sir," Sam replied. "I wonder how a person took a bath."

The professor was inching down the gangplank. "I'd rather not think about it. Come on, there are a lot more stops on the list she gave us."

From there they headed toward the Rock, only a block away. The professor walked slowly but finally they reached it. They leaned over the marble railing to look down upon the famous hunk of granite. The year "1620" had been painted on it and candy wrappers were lying all around.

"There must be a candy machine around here somewhere," the professor said hopefully.

A young man dressed in a Pilgrim outfit was giving a speech to a crowd of tourists. He told how in 1620 the *Mayflower* had anchored offshore and the Pilgrims had come ashore in a longboat, landing right here on the famous rock. His words rang out: "And that is how our brave forefathers arrived here. Are there any questions?"

Sam decided to speak up. "I've been wondering why they would steer toward this boulder when there's a sandy beach on each side."

The college boy stared blankly for a second. Then, ignoring Sam's question, he whipped off his big wide-brimmed hat and held it out upside down. "All right, folks, donations here. Step lively. Make room for others."

When the tourists saw the big hat, they turned and began to push out toward the street. Sam and the professor followed. They returned to the safari wagon and drove up the main street to Mullins House, the only building left of those built during the colony's first years. Its walls were made of mud and sticks and the floor was clean-swept earth. Inside the house there were uncomfortable wooden chairs and a small bed, a huge fireplace where pots and kettles were hanging, and a revolving stand that held picture postcards, five for a dollar.

After they had gone through the old house, Sam

27

and the professor continued their tour, stopping only for hot dogs and potato chips at a lunch counter. Sam had to admit that Miss Tinkerton had been right — a trip to Plymouth could teach a person an awful lot about the Pilgrims and what it was like to have lived in the colony in the early days. It had not been easy for the settlers. Sam was shocked to learn at the burial ground that many of the hundred and two passengers had died during the first winter in the New World.

He and the professor stood silently by themselves, looking at the old graves. There were no other tourists in sight now, and a cold feeling ran through Sam as he thought about the bones underfoot. He was thinking so hard that he jumped a mile when he felt something touch his elbow. Turning, he saw an old man with a long gray beard grinning at him. The fellow wore breeches and shoes with silver buckles.

"Want to see the real thing?" he asked.

Professor Pittfall was startled too. "Where on earth did you come from, mister?"

The stranger made no reply but held out a fistful of cards. They each pulled one out and read:

Travel the Tunnel to Yesterday.
Step into the Past.
Money Back if not Completely Satisfied.

"Where is the tunnel?" Sam asked.

The old man pointed. "Over yon hill. Beyond the statue of the Indian chief. You can't miss it."

28

The professor looked at the slip of paper Miss Tinkerton had given him. "It's the last place on the list," he said. "I guess we'd better see it. Then we can get back for a snack."

Saying good-bye to the old man, they piled back into the safari wagon. They drove up the rise, past the statue of the Indian Sachem and down the other side of the hill. Now there were fewer houses and not so many people. Without all the horns honking and tourists shouting, Sam relaxed.

The wagon crossed an old one-lane bridge over a fairly wide brook. A sign pointed downstream: *To the Tunnel to Yesterday*. Then they went through a wooded section and reached a palisade so high that nothing but the tops of some tall trees could be seen on the other side. After parking, they walked through a wide gate, where they were surprised to meet the same old fellow who had given them the cards.

"Greetings, friends," he grinned. "That will be one dollar each, pray."

Sam looked around. A high fence surrounded them on all sides. The brook ran past and into a large wooden structure just ahead—the Tunnel to Yesterday. Its entrance was framed by wooden posts painted with red and blue stripes. In front of the entrance there was a platform with a small dock to one side where several canoes were tied.

"One dollar," the old fellow repeated, holding out two tickets. "You won't be sorry."

But the professor had spotted the canoes. "My

29

good man, do you really expect me to climb into one of those rickety craft? It would sink in a second."

The old man paused, looking the big archeologist up and down. "Prithee, sir, perhaps you had better meet your young friend at the other end. As soon as I shove him off, I shall return to give you directions."

Sam looked questioningly at the professor, who said, "All right, you go ahead. Then we can report back to the boss that we saw everything."

His curiosity boiling, Sam was eager to go. He dug a bill out of his pocket and handed it to the old man, who led him over to the dock. The canoes were made of real birch bark.

"Are you a swimmer?"

Sam nodded that he was.

"Get in, then."

Sam stepped into the canoe, sat down amidships on a comfortable cushion and picked up a paddle. The old man gave the boat a shove. "Just follow your nose," he said.

The canoe floated toward the entrance to the tunnel, which seemed terribly dark in the bright sunshine. It went gliding past the red and blue posts—and all at once Sam was swallowed up in blackness.

4. THE TUNNEL

AS THE DAYLIGHT at the tunnel entrance fell farther behind, the darkness grew until it became so thick that Sam could barely see the knuckles of his hand on the end of the paddle. He hoped his eyes would adjust to the dark but they didn't. In addition to the gloom, there was total silence except for the bubbling of the stream that carried him along. He steered with the paddle, keeping the canoe from turning sideways.

A slight breeze on his cheek told him that he was moving forward. He closed his eyes. He opened them. No difference. This was the blackest of the black. Sam leaned back against the soft cushion and relaxed. When the canoe bumped against the shore, he paddled and brought it into the stream again. Just when he was wishing he could get his dollar back, he was startled by a flash of light on his left. An amazing scene opened up on the shore. Dimly and softly lit, it showed a group of men, women and children on their knees around a tree. No, it wasn't a tree. As Sam looked more carefully, he realized that it was a ship's mast. The main deck of the *Mayflower!*

The canoe bumped into the bank and hung there while the stream curved around to the right. The figures on the shore were silent. Then a voice was heard from a hidden speaker.

"When the *Mayflower* arrived in the New World, the tired voyagers fell to their knees to thank God for a safe passage across the sea."

Sam strained his eyes to see more closely in the dim light. The group was dressed in the clothing of the 1600s. The men wore outfits like that of the fellow who had sold Sam his ticket. No one moved. They were wax figures. But they looked so real! Sam was astonished.

When the narrator had finished, the lights went out and the Tunnel to Yesterday was returned to blackness and silence. The *Mayflower* scene had been set up in an area along the bank where the waterway took a sharp turn. The canoe had rested there out of the current while Sam watched the show.

Now, with a few strokes of the paddle, he sent the canoe moving again. Pretty soon, as he had expected, he bumped at another right-angle turn. The canoe hugged the shore while lights went up and another tableau came into view. This time he saw a group of men who were armed with muskets and swords. The narrator spoke.

"Captain Myles Standish was in command. He and his men found a good place to build a town at the mouth of a stream of fresh water."

The lights went out. Sam paddled into the current again and leaned back against the cushions. Just as the old man had promised, the Tunnel to Yesterday was interesting and worth a dollar. He watched for the next tableau. It showed the ship's longboat landing at Plymouth Rock.

"Sunday was a day of worship. The following day the Pilgrims came ashore. The men started to build homes. The women did the laundry, and from then on, Monday was always wash day in the New World."

And so the birch-bark canoe went on down the tunnel, one scene after another telling its story and then disappearing into the gloom. Sam saw people building, planting and harvesting. He even saw the first Thanksgiving. Then he stretched out comfortably, gently moving the paddle to keep on course. Now let Miss Tinkerton throw questions at him. He was ready. He knew the history of Plymouth Colony.

As the canoe went deeper into the tunnel, he stopped wondering why there were no other tourists within hearing distance. He didn't care. The tunnel seemed suddenly damp and cold. He shivered and wished he had brought his sweater. But he forgot about that when he came to a scene that was more interesting than any of the others. The lights went up to reveal a band of Indians. Once again Sam was startled at how lifelike the wax figures were. They were engaged in some sort of ceremony, dancing in a circle around a fire. They wore leggins but were bare above the waist. One of

33

them, however, had on a costume that included a headdress of feathers and a deerskin jacket decorated with wampum. His leggins and moccasins were covered with multicolored beads. The narrator's voice was heard.

"The Naugawump Indians ask their god, Keewaytin, for success in a forthcoming hunting and fishing trip."

The Indians chanted, *"Neeshun keesuquit! Keewaytin! Utch kukketaff ktamonk, ktamonk, ktamonk. . . ."*

Who was the fellow in the fancy costume staring into the fire? He must be a medicine man. Why hadn't the narrator mentioned him? He was certainly the finest of all the wax figures in the entire tunnel. Sam was amazed that anyone could make a dummy that looked so much like a real person.

Then the medicine man's head moved slightly.

Sam sat up. "Hey!"

His cry echoed against the walls of the tunnel. The sound surprised the Indian and he moved again. He was not a wax figure! The Indian froze once more but this time he was facing Sam. Only for a moment, though. His eyes opened wide, his jaw dropped and he yelled hoarsely, "You!"

Me? What was going on? Was this a part of the show? Sam was puzzled. He put his paddle into the water.

Now the Indian was angry. He raised his tomahawk.

"Boy! Bring back the numkonk! Return it to our tribe! Splashing Beaver speaks!"

The enraged Naugawump took a step toward Sam. His face and hands were painted with bright colors that gave him a fierce appearance. Behind him the other wax figures remained still. What is the matter with this guy, Sam wondered. What's a numkonk? He started back-paddling just as the howling medicine man charged.

The narrator's calm voice spoke again. "And these are the friendly native Americans who helped our ancestors."

The Naugawump took three steps at full speed to the edge of the stream and leaped into the air. Paddling furiously, Sam looked up to see the maddened fellow flying toward him.

Just then the lights went out.

Sam could see nothing. There was a great splash as the Indian hit the water. At the same time, one end of the canoe was tossed into the air. Now Sam was really scared. The crazy fellow had grabbed the rear end of the fragile craft. He could chop it to pieces in a moment with that mighty tomahawk.

Sam scrambled to his knees in the center of the canoe and dug his paddle into the water. He had to get away. The canoe tipped dangerously. He worked frantically but he seemed to be moving backward. The Indian was pulling the canoe toward shore, letting out yells of mad laughter all the while.

Sam was getting nowhere fast. He must make the medicine man let go of the boat. Lifting the paddle, he swung it blindly behind him and felt it slap hard against something.

There was a shriek. "Ow!" He had hit the attacker. He swung again and again, until suddenly he felt the canoe right itself. He was free! Quickly he took powerful strokes with the paddle and the canoe shot ahead. Sam couldn't see where he was going but it didn't matter as long as he was out of reach of the maddened Naugawump.

Finally the howls faded away and Sam heard nothing but the babbling of the brook. He fell back onto the cushions, breathless, his heart pounding. The old Pilgrim was right—a trip through the tunnel was an unforgettable experience. His head throbbed and his ears rang as the blood rushed through his body. Too exhausted to paddle, he let the canoe drift.

Slowly a grayness filtered into the gloom. Sam saw daylight up ahead. Gently the stream carried him out into the bright sunshine, which hurt his eyes so much that he had to cover them with his hands and peek through his fingers.

When he felt the canoe being pulled aside, he squinted up and saw the face of the old Pilgrim who had sent him on his journey. "Enjoy yourself?" the man asked as he tied up the canoe.

"Sure, but what's the big idea of—" Sam hesitated.

"Of what? You don't wish your money back, do you?"

Sam turned and looked at the cave from which

the stream was flowing peacefully. He had gone right through the hill, past all those interesting wax figures. Where was the mad Naugawump? Inside, waiting for another tourist? Or was there a mad Naugawump after all? Sam inspected the canoe. No sign of damage. Just some water in the bottom. It might have been there from the start.

A few tourists were reloading their cameras and chatting calmly about the tableaux they'd seen. A canoe emerged from the tunnel and a man and woman climbed out. They sure didn't look as though a wild Indian had attacked them. Sam walked slowly toward the exit in the big fence, wondering.

The professor was seated in his safari wagon in the parking lot, eating an apple. He smiled and waved. "That didn't take long. Was it worth it?"

But as the boy hopped into the wagon, the archeologist's smile faded. "What's the matter? You look as though you've seen a ghost."

Sam didn't reply. What could he say? One of the wax figures had come to life? An Indian named Splashing Beaver had chased him with a tomahawk? What would the professor think if he told a crazy story like that? And Miss Tinkerton. They would probably send him back to Junction City on the next bus and search around for someone with more sense to take his place.

Finally Sam found his voice. "No, no ghosts. It's just a very real show, that's what. Like going back three hundred years. I wish you'd been there with me." He meant that.

"Maybe we'll put pontoons on old Lulu here someday and drive through. Otherwise, forget it."

"By the way, Professor," Sam asked, "what is a numkonk?"

"Numkonk? I don't know. A kind of shell, perhaps. Why do you ask?"

"Oh, nothing. Just curious."

The professor started the engine. "Here, have an apple."

Sam munched slowly and thoughtfully all the way home.

5. THE SECRET

DINNER WAS by candlelight in Tinkerton Manor's big dining room. Diggins stood at the sideboard, slicing another helping of roast beef for Professor Pittfall. Sam talked about his experiences in Plymouth, carefully leaving out any mention of Splashing Beaver. He tried to tell himself that he had fallen asleep in the canoe, that the attack had been a nightmare. But deep inside he felt it might have been more than that. It had been so real. It was a puzzle he would have to solve by himself, one way or another, even if it meant getting up enough nerve to go back through the Tunnel to Yesterday.

Miss Tinkerton interrupted his thoughts. "My word, Samuel, you seem to have learned more than I had hoped for. I am so glad because it is important that when you dig into the past, you know all you can about the early days."

Professor Pittfall's chair creaked as he cut his meat. "Mighty fine food," he declared between bites. "Reminds me of the excellent meals of the famous Oracle Restaurant on the summit of Mount

Olympus. You could show them a thing or two, Elvira."

"Why, thank you, Potter, but be sure to give Diggins some credit too. He is my assistant chef, you know. Will you have some more Yorkshire pudding?"

"Don't mind if I do." He passed his plate.

Sam had eaten his fill. His mind was racing with excitement because they would start their work in the morning.

"This dig is going to be like a real mystery," he said. "We don't know what we're looking for. Nobody knows what's inside Queppish Hill."

Miss Tinkerton was silent for a moment. The only sound was made by the professor as he chewed the crisp Yorkshire pudding. Then she spoke quietly. "There is more to the story than I have told you."

The professor looked up at her. "Well, Elvira, if it's important, get on with it."

"Back in sixteen twenty," she began, "the first Tinkerton arrived in Plymouth on the *Mayflower* with his wife and son John. Then something happened that made the Pilgrims banish the Tinkertons from the colony. They settled on this property, right where we are now. The family was in disgrace for a century or more, until people gradually forgot about it. But the Tinkertons never forgot. When I was a young woman, I heard there was a curse on us but my family would never talk about it. I stayed away from Plymouth because I felt guilty but I didn't know why. And I still feel that way."

She paused and looked down. It wasn't easy for her to tell the story. She straightened up and went on.

"Then a few years ago when my father died, he whispered the secret to me on his deathbed."

"What was it?" Sam asked.

She stood up. "Come with me, please."

"Dessert," the professor murmured.

"Diggins will serve us in the library."

They followed her into the other room, where a fire blazed in the hearth. She reached above the mantel and pressed a panel that popped open, revealing a safe. Twiddling the dial, she opened its door and took out a flimsy brown parchment, rolled up and tied with a leather strap. She set it on the table before them.

"Be careful," she warned. "It's old."

"It surely is." The professor took out his magnifying glass to inspect it. "What's inside?"

"It's too fragile to unroll but I know what it says. Papa told me." She took a deep breath. "It charges my ancestor, John Tinkerton, with kidnapping and suspicion of murder and banishes the family from Plymouth."

"Gosh," Sam breathed. "Why didn't they just lock him up?"

"They didn't have a prison then," the professor pointed out, "so they sent him away with his parents. To be exiled like that was a terrible punishment."

"He was only a kid, wasn't he?" Sam asked.

"About your age," Miss Tinkerton said.

"Who did he kidnap and maybe murder? And why?" Sam asked.

"If Papa knew, he didn't tell me. He just said that the body was never found. As it turned out, of course, the punishment wasn't so terrible after all. The Tinkertons got this fine property. The family prospered over the years. Today we have this mansion and the estate. And yet the Tinkerton Curse has been hanging over our heads for more than three centuries."

Carefully she put the parchment away in the safe and closed the panel. "Papa told me to forget about it but now I want to go one step further. I have a funny feeling that John Tinkerton never hurt anyone and I hope to prove it."

The professor raised his eyebrows. "A funny feeling? Is that all?"

"There are no criminals in our family history as far as I have been able to learn. All of our people have been honest and hardworking. If John had been such a bad person, wouldn't there have been other Tinkertons like him? Well, there were not."

"That makes sense," the professor admitted.

She clenched her fists. "Of course it makes sense. I have searched high and low to prove I'm right, without success. Now the only place left to look into is Queppish Hill and when you two explorers dig into it, you'll find the evidence that will rid my family of the Tinkerton Curse for good. I'm sure of it!"

6. THE DIG

SAM AND THE PROFESSOR worked six days a week. "This job must be finished this summer," their employer insisted. "That's what I'm paying you for." She did give them Sundays off, though.

After eating a hearty breakfast, they would climb into Lulu and drive the mile to Queppish Hill, where Sam would take up the spade. Keeping within the narrow path marked out by stakes and strings, he would dig straight into the side of the hill. The deeper he went, the more dirt he had to take out. There was no place to put it as the hill rose ahead and on both sides of him. So he would pile it into two buckets standing behind him. When they were full, he would carry them to a big screen and dump them. By shaking the screen, the dirt would fall through but everything else was caught. The professor would throw out weeds, roots and rocks and look over whatever was left.

The screen had to be moved to a new spot once a day because the dirt piled up beneath it. The professor said this was the best way to sift through ancient ruins and not miss something important.

The soil was sandy and soft but still the shoveling was hard work. Sam itched from poison ivy in a few places and even though he wore gloves, his hands blistered. Miss Tinkerton treated him for these problems but she didn't tell him to slow down with his work. Professor Pittfall wasn't any help because he never could have squeezed into the narrow passage. So Sam just kept on digging, looking forward to the exciting discoveries he hoped were ahead.

Also, he was learning a lot about archeology. The professor always explained the reason for every little move and he talked about his digs in other parts of the world. In the evenings at the manor house, he often described his adventures.

One day they shook the screen and the professor pounced upon a narrow little stone with a point. "Eureka!"

"What is it?" Sam asked.

The professor turned the object over and over, rubbing it clean. "An arrowhead of the Algonquin nation."

"Is that good?"

"You bet your booties it is." He held the arrowhead up so the sun flashed on it. "When we get back tonight, I'll go through my books and find out exactly which tribe this belonged to. You're doing great, lad. Keep up the good work."

Later they sipped tea and looked out at the sailboats on the waters of Tinkerton Sea. The professor talked about the old days. "You know,

Sam, this is a lovely place and a fine time of year for digging. It reminds me of my first expedition. It was in the Poona Islands and I was a mere lad of about your age. Lord Burwell, one of the great explorers of the time, was searching for the missing link that would prove that the Poona Islanders had really come from Kittakorn centuries ago, crossing the Straits of Rappledor. I'll never forget the day we found that ancient Kittakorn map, carved in stone, in the deserted Poona temple deep in the jungle. What excitement! His Lordship gave each of us a gold piece as a reward."

"Maybe we'll make a great discovery like that too," Sam ventured.

He didn't mind the blisters so much after that, now that there was something to show for them. It was fun to wonder what would turn up next on the screen. As the days passed, the table in front of the tent held more and more items: arrowheads, spearheads, a broken clay bowl, fishhooks and many other little relics. The professor studied these things and soon announced that Queppish Hill was once the home of the Naugawump Indian tribe.

Miss Tinkerton was not happy, though.

"This isn't what I'm looking for," she complained on one of her visits to the site.

"I can't help that, Elvira," the professor replied. "We are only doing our job. What kind of sandwiches have you brought?"

She plumped the picnic basket on the table. "Cream cheese and jelly on pumpernickel. Watercress on white."

The professor quickly lifted the basket off the table. "Careful, you might damage the artifacts we've dug up."

"Damage them?" she snorted. "They're nothing but a bunch of broken stones and old bones."

Professor Pittfall hoisted himself from his chair. "My dear Elvira, sit down and let me explain something to you."

While Sam spread the picnic cloth on the ground and set out the lunch, the professor soothed Miss Tinkerton. This was only the beginning, he told her. The discovery of Indian relics meant that Queppish Hill had a history. It could be Tinkerton history as well as Naugawump history. The only way to get at the facts was to keep on digging. He gave her quite a lesson in archeology.

At last she seemed satisfied. That night at dinner she said cheerfully, "I am really quite pleased with your work, gentlemen, now that I understand it better. Tomorrow is Saturday. Why don't you take the afternoon off? There's a wonderful double feature at the Nickelodeon in Falmouth. After supper, Diggins can drive us down and I'll treat you."

Sam smiled at the thought but Professor Pittfall seemed to be thinking it over.

"They have a big popcorn machine," she added, "and an ice-cream-and-candy counter."

"I'll go," the archeologist said.

Even though it rained, Sam enjoyed the weekend. He went back to work on Monday morning full of

47

energy. His and the professor's dirty clothes had been turned over to the washerwoman and today he was wearing fresh jeans and a clean shirt. Professor Pittfall's spotless khaki shorts had been ironed, at his request.

The rain had washed some soil into the passageway but Sam quickly cleared it away and dug deeper than ever into Queppish Hill. Another bone fishhook turned up but in the afternoon, after lunch, there was a really big surprise. With a clang, the spade struck something hard.

"Stop!" the professor ordered when he heard the sound. "It may be important." From the safari wagon he took two small brushes and a trowel. "Use these, and don't hurt whatever it is."

As Sam gently brushed and scraped the hard object, he could see that it was a granite rock about the size of a basketball but rather square. He dug along each side of it, above and below, and found similar boulders.

"Well, I'll be King Tut's mummy!" exclaimed the professor, squeezing into the passageway as far as he could. "What have we here?"

"Looks to me like a stone wall," Sam said.

"You could be right, son. Let's find out."

He went to the safari wagon again and this time returned with a long, thin rod of metal, which he told Sam to poke into the hill. Sam did. He poked all around the area of the boulders. He hit more of the same hard stone. The professor, who had written down everything that happened from the first day, took out his notebook and made a sketch

48

of the stones. He then studied the sketch, the hill, the sketch again, and. asked, "Do you notice something?"

Sam looked over the professor's shoulder. "What?"

"The boulders lean toward the center."

They walked around the mound, inspecting it carefully. When they returned to the tent, the professor nodded his head. "Unexpected, but not surprising. If I am not mistaken, this is not a hill but an Algonquin storehouse built of stone and covered with a heavy layer of dirt and sand. The Naugawumps belonged to the Algonquin nation, you know. The hill should be hollow inside. The entrance will be somewhere on the top, far removed from the place you have been digging up for the last two weeks."

Sam groaned. "Gee whiz."

"Not to worry. We have already made some remarkable discoveries."

"But if there's an entrance on top, how can we find it? I can't dig up all that dirt."

"No problem, my boy. We shall resort to the ancient art of rhabdomancy."

"The what?"

"Dowsing." The professor rummaged around in the wagon and took out a slim, V-shaped stick.

"I know something about dowsing," Sam said, "but I thought it was for finding water."

"Oh, it is. And this very same divining rod, made from the green twig of the pampong tree that grows only on the slopes of the Mountains of the Moon in

49

Africa—this very divining rod showed me the way to the underground lakes of Constantinople when all else had failed. But it also gives its user the power to find other hidden treasures—fabulous jewelry, secret scrolls, sunken galleons." He held the ends of the wand in his fists, palms up, the V part in the center pointing ahead.

"How does it work?" Sam asked.

"It's very puzzling," the professor said. "To put it simply, every animal, vegetable or mineral gives off its own special aura in the form of invisible waves. At the same time, the alpha waves from the brain of the dowser surge down through his or her fingers. Now, let's say the wand is picking up the aura of the rocks underneath Queppish Hill. Suddenly it picks up a different aura, like an opening or a door. It will twist and turn when your alpha waves feel the difference. Is that clear?"

"I'm not sure. Maybe if I saw it in action, I would understand."

"See it in action? No, Sam, you're going to do it in action. I can't climb to the top of that hill and so it's up to you to dowse it and find the entrance into this mysterious mound."

7. WONDERFUL THINGS

SAM STOOD on the top of Queppish Hill, grasping the ends of the wand in his upturned fists. A few minutes of coaching by the professor had told him all he had to know about dowsing but he still wasn't sure of himself. He glanced nervously at the archeologist, standing at ground level, who called up to him, "Just remember — you have to *believe*."

Sam didn't move. He closed his eyes, gently squeezed the slender pampong branch and tried to believe.

"Go on, Sam. Start dowsing."

He drew a deep breath, looked down and slowly moved forward, step by step. The top of the hill was about as long and as wide as the Tinkerton tennis court but it was slightly humped in the center, not quite flat. He worked his way back and forth, kicking his feet through the weeds, baby pines and shrubs.

"Not too tight, not too loose," the professor warned. "Remember, you'll feel it in your thumbs, or maybe in your palms."

Sam concentrated as hard as he could, trying to shut out all other thoughts and sounds. He imagined that magical waves were flowing back and forth between his brain and the mysterious mound. As he went along, he did begin to feel a tingling in his fingers but the V point of the dowsing rod was still pointing straight ahead.

He felt sure the secret opening was there beneath him somewhere, and he felt sure the wand would find it. He knew how important it was to believe. Back and forth he went, slow step by slow step, up across the mound, turning around and going back on a slightly different path. He had covered almost half the top and was near the exact center of the hump when the message came. The tingling in his fingers shot up his arms and the shiny green pampong stick twisted a bit.

Sam caught his breath and halted. "It moved! It's pointing!"

"Keep going," the professor called out, "until it tells you exactly where to dig."

Sam took another step. The rod squirmed and pointed directly at his feet.

"It's here! We've found it!"

"Good boy. Mark it carefully and then get your pick and shovel. Forget about filling the buckets. Just dig."

Sam followed orders, tossing the dirt to one side. He had dug a hole about two feet deep and twice as wide when the pick struck something hard.

The professor heard the sound. "What's that?"

Sam cleared away more dirt. "It looks like wood. A trapdoor maybe. It has a leather handle."

"Okay, lift it up and let's see what's inside."

"I can't. It's stuck."

"Gadzooks! We'll have to set up a windlass."

From the safari wagon the professor pulled out some two-by-fours and ropes, clamps, bolts and tools. He had Sam carry this equipment onto the hill and then he shouted directions up to him.

In about an hour's time Sam had put together a sturdy windlass right over the hole. Lowering one end of the rope, he hooked it to the trapdoor handle. Then he cranked the windlass until the timber cover was raised and could be dragged off to the side. Clinging to a leg of the windlass frame to keep from falling in, he leaned over to look down. A little sunlight came in over his shoulder but not enough to reveal much of the inside of the hill.

"What do you see?" the professor yelled.

"Nothing. It's black as night in there and it smells awful."

"The ladder. The searchlight," the professor called out. "Come and get them. And bring the end of the rope with you."

Sam scrambled down the hill, pulling the windlass rope with him. The explorer grabbed it and tied it securely around his big waist. "I'll bring the light," he said. "You fetch the ladder."

The ladder was hanging along Lulu's side. Sam unhooked it and dragged it atop the hill and then looked down at the professor. "Now crank the windlass handle," Pittfall ordered, grasping the rope with one hand and holding the light in the other.

When the windlass handle was turned, the rope tightened and pulled as the professor climbed up the side of Queppish Hill. Step by step, leaning forward, he inched his body along. His face grew red and he puffed. Sam strained at the windlass until, with a final grunt, the professor reached the top, where he could walk by himself.

"Whew!" He dropped the rope, grinned at Sam and looked around. "What a beautiful view of Tinkerton Sea. There's the yacht club on the other side." Picking his way over to where Sam had been digging, he peered down. The silent and black hole stared back at him.

"Let's let the ladder down," he said.

They lowered it between the legs of the windlass until it struck bottom. The professor tested the searchlight and held it out to Sam, who fidgeted and said, "I don't think I want to be the first one down there."

The professor seemed surprised. "Why not? Surely you're not afraid of the dark at your age."

"No, sir."

"There's certainly no living thing down there that could harm you. You know I'd go if I could squeeze through the small entrance. Take this with you and it'll be like daylight in there."

"It's a good searchlight," Sam stalled, "but—"

"Just think, you'll be the first to step foot inside this ancient place for many years. Maybe you'll get the same thrill Sir Flinders Petrie did when he opened the tomb of King Tut. You want to be an archeologist, remember? Let me tell you, Sam, this is what it's all about. The excitement of discovery. You ought to jump at the chance."

Suddenly Sam felt foolish. "Give me that light." He stepped onto the top rung of the ladder and started down. "Here goes."

"Good boy. Watch your step."

Slowly he descended into the blackness. A blast of stale air beat against his face and entered his lungs. He stopped, feeling slightly dizzy, his heart pounding. He aimed the light at the dirt floor. It looked safe enough to step on. When he finally landed, he shone the light around. The sight made him cry out, "Wow!"

The professor's voice came from above. "What do you see?"

"I see wonderful things," Sam said.

8. A TERRIBLE CRIME

THE INSIDE of the mound was a large chamber built of stones like those Sam had come up against while digging into the side of the hill. With the flashlight he could see only sections of it at a time but from what he could make out there were shelves and benches around the walls. In the shelves, on the benches and in cubbyholes there were statues, masks, pots, bowls, shells and a lot of other items that seemed old and strange to him.

Here and there spears, paddles and shields were leaning against the walls. The dirt floor was packed hard and one end of the chamber sloped down into a shallow pit. Stone columns supported the roof, which seemed to be made of large timbers. The beams would have to be strong to hold up all that dirt piled on top. Sam described everything to the professor, who leaned over the opening, peering down.

"Sam, my boy," he exclaimed, "a veritable treasure trove of antiquities! We must bring these priceless relics out into the daylight so we can identify them."

Down came a basket, lowered by the rope of the windlass. In it were a kerosene lamp and matches.

"Start sending things up," the professor ordered, "but do it carefully."

Sam lit the lamp and set it on the floor at his feet. It was not much better than the searchlight but at least he could use two hands now. Standing there in the dark, clammy place, he felt a chill run through his body. The lamp's dim light cast shadows that flickered on the spooky masks hanging on the walls. They seemed to move and roll their eyes, to grin at him. He tried to shake off the dizziness he felt.

This is silly, he thought. Masks can't move. Their eyes are just holes in the wood. The funny feeling must be from the stale air he was breathing. The professor's voice brought him back to his senses. "Okay, we're ready."

Sam stepped over to one of the masks and gently lifted it from its resting place. Carved of wood, its colors faded, it had openings that the wearer could see and talk through. Leather thongs could be used to tie it at the back of the head. It seemed to be in good condition, considering how old it was. It was the face of an angry Indian. There was a scary look to it in the dark. Sam placed it in the basket. The professor hauled it up and let out cries of pleasure.

"Marvelous! Send more!"

The next few basket-loads carried another mask, a soapstone statue of an animal, a pipe carved in the shape of a frog, a tomahawk, spoons, a necklace made of shells, a spear and many other interesting

57

odds and ends. It was late afternoon when the professor called a halt. Sam was glad to quit because he was tired and he also felt funny from breathing the stale air. The last thing he sent up was a heavy crock that was too big to fit into the basket. He just tied the rope around it and it was hauled up by itself. Then he grabbed one of the shields, climbed up the ladder and stepped out into the fresh air and daylight.

They carried their discoveries down the hill and spread them out on the table in front of the tent. The professor grinned and shook his head in amazement.

"And just think, there's a lot more down there," Sam said.

"This will keep us busy. We'll have to tag each item, record it and maybe even photograph the important ones."

"Yup, that's archeology," Sam smiled.

"And now let's see. We ought to take back something to show Elvira. What's in here?" The professor lifted the lid off the big earthen crock. "Looks like handmade stuff. Put this in the safari wagon, if you please."

Sam did as he was asked. Then they tied a cloth cover over the things on the table, climbed into Lulu and drove back to the manor, feeling pleased with the day's work.

At dinner Miss Tinkerton was quite fascinated by the news. "Does this mean we're on the right track?" she asked.

Professor Pittfall explained that there were still a lot more relics within the hill and that everything would have to be removed, sorted out and studied. "We have to move carefully, Elvira. I don't wish to jump to any conclusions."

"I understand, Potter. I'm so very impatient, that's all."

He folded his napkin and got up from the table. "A fine repast. Now, for a starter, let us take a look at the big earthen crock."

Sam was disappointed. It was filled with dust and flat hunks of clay. "Looks like garbage."

"Not so fast," said the professor, brushing dust from one of the clay pieces and examining it with his magnifying glass. "See all those scratches on the surface? Hieroglyphics, my boy."

Sam counted a hundred and twenty-one clay tablets when they were all cleaned off and spread out on the library table. Each one had marks on both sides that looked to him like hen tracks.

"Higher what?" he asked.

"Hieroglyphics," the professor explained. "It's Algonquin, a mixture of pictures and letters and signs. The Algonquins had their own written language, you know, unlike other Indian tribes. They would write in the soft clay and then it would harden and last forever, like these tablets."

"What do they say?" Miss Tinkerton asked.

Sam looked at a tablet through the magnifying glass. *Ch&gsh. Ahm&nook&k.* A tiny picture of a fishhead maybe, or was it a spear? Nothing made any sense.

"Ah," breathed the professor in answer to Miss Tinkerton's question, "that is for us to find out. I shall take out my Algonquin dictionary tonight and translate."

But it wasn't that simple. The great explorer-archeologist stayed up late, comparing the writing on the tablets with drawings and letters in his big book. The others finally went up to bed, leaving him to his task.

At breakfast he was unhappy. "An ancient Naugawump dialect, I'm sorry to say."

"You cannot translate it?" Miss Tinkerton asked glumly.

"Not well enough to be of use."

"Gosh," Sam said, "it might have told us all about the old stone chamber."

The professor clapped his hands. "A minor setback, my friends. I shall not give up. Come on, partner, back to work. There is much to be done."

As Lulu jounced through the pine woods toward Queppish Hill, Sam was not looking forward to spending another day inside its gloomy walls, breathing that foul air and imagining that spooks were about to tap him on the shoulder. As it turned out, he didn't go down the ladder that day. When they lifted the cover off the table in front of the tent, Sam's jaw dropped in surprise and the professor cried, "What on earth has been going on here?"

At least half of the relics they had taken from the stone chamber were missing.

"We've been robbed!" Sam exclaimed.

It was unbelievable. Who would want these ancient things? They couldn't be sold easily. And how did thieves find out so quickly that the objects were there on the table? Queppish Hill was hidden deep in the woods. Had someone come along in a boat and watched the men while they worked? Sam didn't remember seeing anyone else in the area.

"This is outrageous," the professor said angrily. "Look for tracks. They must have had a vehicle of some sort."

But there were no signs—no tire tracks, no footprints. They searched the woods and even waded into Tinkerton Sea, thinking that maybe pranksters had thrown the things into the water. No luck.

Satisfied that the stolen items were not to be found nearby, they hurried back to the manor. Horrified, Miss Tinkerton called the sheriff's office. It took up most of the day for the sheriff to arrive, to inspect the scene and to make a list of the missing relics. When he finally left, he promised to do his best to solve the crime.

The threesome sat unhappily in the library while tea was served. "Gee," Sam said, "I hope those crooks don't come back and swipe the rest of our stuff."

"They won't," the professor declared, "because you and I are going to guard it. We're going to sleep in the tent every night from now on."

9. A PROWLER

EVEN THOUGH it was dark when Sam woke up, he could see his watch. A quarter past ten. The professor was still on guard, then. He could be heard stirring about outside the tent. Something else could be heard too—heavy breathing from the other cot. The professor was snoring. How could he be snoring in his cot if—? Sam's heart seemed to jump into his throat. His eyes stared toward the tent flap. He could see nothing but the dark. What was that noise? Was it an animal rooting after the lunch leftovers? Or had the thief returned?

Sam had gone to sleep fully dressed except for his sneakers, which he now slowly and quietly pulled on his feet. He reached out and put a hand on the shoulder of the professor, who let out a snort, rolled over and kept on snoring. Sam shook him gently but the man was a sound sleeper. Some watchman! Sam groped for the searchlight. He and the professor had decided that if the thief were once frightened away, he would not return. But if they wanted to retrieve the stolen goods, they would have to capture the culprit or at least get a look at him so they could describe him to the sheriff.

Nervously Sam stuck his head out the tent door, aimed the light in the direction of the table and pressed the switch. The bright beam stabbed through the darkness. No thief was in sight but the cover had been pulled aside and a lot more of the precious relics were gone. As he moved the light back and forth, he heard noises from the direction of Queppish Hill.

"Hey, Professor Pittfall!" he shouted. "Quick, before he gets away!"

He went after the thief, shining the beam of light here and there as he circled the mound. But he wasn't fast enough. The intruder had disappeared into the woods. No telling which way he had gone. There was no point in blindly charging off after him. Sam turned back to meet the professor when something caught his eye at the top of the mound. A dim light was flickering over parts of the windlass. It must be coming from the inside of the stone chamber. So the thief was in there, hiding.

Sam scrambled to the top of the hill, wishing the professor would hurry up and help. Reaching the entrance, he looked down and saw flames. Was the robber setting fire to the ancient relics? A puff of smoke caught him in the face, choking him, watering his eyes. He coughed, began to rub his eyes and dropped the searchlight, which clattered down the ladder. Sam reached for it, lost his balance and started to fall. Grabbing the rungs, he held on but his grip was too weak. Slowly he slid feet-first, thumpety-thump, right down into a heap on the floor of the stone chamber.

Groggy, on his hands and knees, he gasped for breath and choked on the smoke and rotten air. That old dizzy feeling came over him, only worse this time. He couldn't stand up. Raising his head, he saw a small fire burning in the pit at one end of the room and behind it there was a sight that gave him goose pimples. A dark, strangely dressed figure stared back at him from behind the spooky mask that Sam had removed from the wall the day before. The flickering light of the fire made it seem even spookier. And there was something familiar about the stranger.

"You—you thief!" Sam croaked through a dry throat. "You robbed us!"

The stranger took off the mask and retorted angrily, "The medicine man of the Naugawumps does not rob. You are the robber. Look about you."

He stepped back from the fire and pointed to the walls. But Sam could not take his eyes off the thief's face. That outfit—deerskin leggins, jacket, beads. Where had he seen it before? The Tunnel to Yesterday!

"Splashing Beaver!" he cried out.

Stunned, he turned his gaze away. The flickering light of the fire dimly lit the walls but it was enough for him to see that the shelves, benches and cubbyholes were filled again. The stolen relics had been put back.

"Where is the numkonk?" the Indian demanded.

So that was it. This crazy guy was still looking for

that, whatever a numkonk might be. Now the medicine man raised his arms over his head, looked upward and chanted, *"Peyaum Keewaytin. Hobomock nummet . . . kuhtah, kuhtah, kuhtah."*

He went on chanting as Sam tried to pull himself together. But the smoke and foul air had gone to the boy's head. He felt faint. The Naugawump reached into a leather pouch and took out a handful of powder which he threw on the fire.

"Sakopagunkum!"

A bright green flame shot up on high, followed by a cloud of smoke that floated across the chamber.

"Pqtchx!" the Indian called out.

Before he could help it, Sam had breathed in several lungsful of the pungent fumes. Still on his hands and knees, he felt himself going, his mind sinking and darkness closing in on him. He fell unconscious.

When Sam awoke, he was lying on his back. It was daytime. His watch said half past ten. What had happened? Had he slept through the whole night? Light was streaming in through the entrance in the roof but the ladder was gone and he couldn't see the windlass either. Why had the professor removed them? In place of the terrible smoke and smell, he was breathing clean, fresh air. His head was clear and he felt good. He was lying on a soft blanket and his head rested on fragrant balsam needles. He climbed to his feet.

He was still inside the stone chamber, but what a change! Splashing Beaver was not there. The fire was out and at one end of the room there was a pool of water. In the daylight he could see the relics on the shelves quite clearly. They seemed more colorful, newer-looking, not as crumbly and dusty as when he last saw them. Most surprising were the small windows around the walls. They let in the light. Sam sprang to one of the openings. It was just big enough for his head. There was no longer a pile of dirt covering the stone chamber. Queppish Hill was gone. He ran from window to window. The tent was gone. Lulu was gone. Instead of a forest of pines outside, he saw oaks and other big trees.

The edge of Tinkerton Sea came right up to the stone chamber. There were no sailboats but two canoes raced each other across the water. Each canoe was paddled by two young Indians.

Now Sam was alarmed. What was going on? He had better get out, he decided. But how? Except for the tiny windows, the only opening was in the roof far above his head. There was nothing high enough for him to stand on to get even close to it. The stone chamber was now a prison. He shouted through one of the windows, "Professor Pittfall! It's me, Sam! Get me out of here!"

One of the canoers glanced his way and then kept on racing. Sam's cries were answered by silence. He waited. He looked at his watch again. Ten-thirty. That's what it had said earlier. He shook it. No use. It was stuck. Battery worn out. Suddenly there was a racket overhead. The ladder was being lowered through the entrance.

"Thank goodness, Professor!" Sam cried. "You finally heard me."

The moment the ladder hit the dirt floor, he had a foot on the bottom rung but before he could start up, someone came down, forcing him aside.

Splashing Beaver!

Sam jumped back against the wall, grabbing one of the spears. He pointed the weapon at the Indian. "Get out of my way!"

But the medicine man stood calmly at the foot of the ladder. In one arm he carried a garment of some sort. In the other hand he held a shiny red object on the end of a leather thong. Smiling, he held it out to Sam.

"Welcome, Hobomock, to the land of the Naugawumps," he said with a warm smile. "Here is your numkonk."

10. THE VILLAGE

A BEWILDERED Sam Churchill looked himself up and down. Over his shoulders he wore a cape woven of thick, long grass and trimmed with colored beads. He had changed from dungarees and sneakers into deerskin leggins and moccasins. Splashing Beaver had tied black and white feathers in Sam's hair and painted his face with colored pigments that had been mixed in little bowls. His own mother wouldn't know him, Sam decided.

And hanging around his neck was—the numkonk! It was nothing more than a big, hollow lobster claw. But it was very important to Splashing Beaver and the Naugawumps. Its surface was covered with writing—hieroglyphics, just as on the clay tablets in the library back at the house.

"It is sacred. Wear it always," the medicine man had said, waving his arm in a circle. "Temple of Keewaytin is also sacred."

For the first time, Sam noticed the pictures of lobsters that were painted on the walls. He smiled, having made up his mind to be as friendly as possible with the Naugawump who had not long ago attacked him with a tomahawk. Now, for some reason, Sam had been all dolled up in a fancy costume and everything was buddy-buddy. That was nice. But—wear it always? Phooey. The minute he got back to Tinkerton Manor, he'd get rid of this junk in a hurry.

But where was Tinkerton Manor? Where was Queppish Hill? Where was the professor? Where am I? Keewaytin. Hobomock. What did those names mean?

"Come," Splashing Beaver ordered. Sam followed him up the ladder, noting that now the rungs were attached with leather thongs, not nails. Reaching the roof, he looked about. The Temple of Keewaytin, was it? Meant for a god of some sort? So this was what had been underneath Queppish Hill all along. There was no sign of the mound of earth he had dug into. No sign of Professor Pittfall, of the tent, of Lulu. The camping and digging permit wasn't tacked on the tree.

There had to be an explanation and for a while Sam thought he had it: He must still be in the Tunnel to Yesterday. He had been knocked unconscious by the Indian's tomahawk and he was dreaming. Why not? He used to have some wild dreams. But this was the wildest. He wished he could wake up.

Splashing Beaver led the way down stone steps built into the outside wall of the temple. Sam followed, the numkonk swinging on the leather thong around his neck. There was only one trouble with the dream theory: All this was much too real. It was no dream. There was another explanation and it was a scary one.

A white birch-bark canoe was drawn up on the beach. Sam climbed in and sat down in the middle while Splashing Beaver shoved off and began to paddle across the water, heading for the opposite shore. Sam knew that from the middle of the sea he could see Tinkerton Manor in the distance, high on its hill beyond the pine forest. When they were halfway out, he turned to look back at it.

It wasn't there.

Now he felt the hairs on the back of his neck stand on end. The disappearance of the manor house fit in with his scary new theory. As the canoe moved closer to the shore, he could see a busy Indian village where there had once been a yacht club. Now he knew his theory was correct: Some powerful force had taken over, setting him down in a different time period. Was it far in the future? Not likely. Everything pointed to times gone by. Although he was Sam Churchill of the twentieth century, right now he was living in the past. How far past? He didn't know the answer but it had to be sometime before Tinkerton Manor and Queppish Hill came on the scene.

How or why this was happening to him, Sam couldn't guess. He did know that he was a part of some scheme of Splashing Beaver's, whose magic had brought him here by way of the stone chamber, the Temple of Keewaytin. And his only way back would be through the temple. It was the connection

70

to the century where he belonged. For now, though, he would have to keep his eyes and ears open and play the medicine man's game. It was his only hope.

The prow of the canoe slid onto the sand. A group of Indian men, women and children was there, waiting to greet the two passengers. As Sam and Splashing Beaver stepped ashore, the Naugawumps fell to their knees, raised their palms to the sky and chanted, *"Neeshun . . . utch . . . kukketaff . . ."* Sam recognized the language. He had heard the medicine man singing those words in the tunnel and in the temple. Without thinking, he happened to put his hand on the numkonk. The chanting grew louder.

He was glad when Splashing Beaver led him away from the group. "Come. We shall meet our Sachem." They walked across the village clearing toward the largest of the dozen houses that faced the sea. The Indians followed, joined by others from the village. Mostly the people hung back but several of the children ran up to touch Sam's cape and dart away, giggling.

The Naugawumps gathered behind Sam and Splashing Beaver as they reached the dwelling, where an old Indian man and a young girl stood awaiting them. They nodded in greeting as the medicine man spoke in his own tongue, introducing Sam. After the old man replied, Splashing Beaver translated his words for Sam.

"The great Sachem Queppish welcomes Hobomock. He also speaks for his daughter,

71

Princess Minnetonka. You bring honor to our people. We are pleased that you take part in the important festival and celebration for Keewaytin, god of the seafish."

Queppish. Well, that was a familiar name to Sam. He raised his right hand in salute and replied, "Greetings!" He touched the sacred lobster claw with his left hand and the Naugawumps were pleased.

The Sachem invited the two visitors into the house, where they sat on the ground while the princess prepared their food. Until then, Sam had not realized how hungry he was. The meal was served in wooden bowls and there were no forks or napkins. He watched the others and did as they did, eating with his fingers and wiping his mouth with the back of his hand. He was surprised that the Indians looked neat and polite even while eating in this way. His mother would never believe it. It takes practice, he decided, as he licked cornmeal mush off his fingers. He had some hard bread and washed it down with a cup of bitter cider. He enjoyed the entire meal.

In the center of the house there was a firepit. Above it a hole went through the roof to let out the smoke. Since the fire was out now, some light came in that way, and some also came through the doorway. But the room was still a bit dark. The house seemed to be made of wooden poles packed with mud and covered with grass matting. There were baskets around the walls for storing household goods.

The Indians ate silently, without hurry, as though they hadn't a care in the world. Sam fidgeted and was happy when Queppish smiled and spoke.

"Neetchy agwonk, Hobomock."

"Queppish asks where Hobomock comes from," Splashing Beaver translated.

"Who is Hobomock — me?" Sam asked.

"Yes."

"You tell him. You know as much about it as I do."

The medicine man replied to the Sachem, who went on to ask many more questions that Sam did his best to answer. How many winters are you? Is your home near water? Does your father hunt or fish? Does he have pale skin too? Is your tribe warlike? Why do you want to make sacrifice to Keewaytin?

Queppish seemed satisfied with whatever it was that Splashing Beaver told him in translation. Finally, when the Sachem fell silent, Sam blurted out, "Now I have a few questions of my own."

"Speak, Hobomock," the medicine man said.

"For one, how come you know the English language and the others don't?"

"I learn many tongues as I pass through the ages."

"Then it's true, as I figured, that I'm in a different time — or something."

"Yes, Hobomock, it is true."

"What time?"

"The time of the Sachem Queppish in the Year of the Cod."

73

"Where?"

"The land of the Naugawumps, the center of the world as we know it."

Sam was annoyed at the answers that didn't tell him what he wanted to know. "But why?" he demanded.

"You rob from the sacred Temple of Keewaytin. You steal the numkonk."

"Steal it!" Sam said angrily. "You gave it to me. Here, you can have it back." He slipped the thong off over his head. The Sachem and the princess cried out in alarm. The villagers outside the door groaned and moaned.

"No, Hobomock," Splashing Beaver warned. "Must not remove numkonk."

Sam let the sacred claw drop around his neck once more. The Indians settled down. "Okay, I'll wear it to make you happy. But let's get something straight. I want out of here real soon. Wipe this paint off my face. Return my clothes. Get out your magic powder and send me back to where I belong."

The medicine man stared Sam in the eye. "This is where you belong. You are Hobomock. Keewaytin wants you. You stay. Understand?"

Sam blinked. He understood. He didn't like it. He was a prisoner.

11. LIFE WITH THE NAUGAWUMPS

SAM SPENT the night in the temple. After getting him settled, Splashing Beaver left some cider and dried fruit and promised to return in the morning. Sam climbed to the top of the ladder and watched him paddle away in the dusk. Now, Sam thought, I can escape. But to where? He sighed and went back down. Might as well get some rest.

He took off the fancy cape, hung the numkonk on a hook, knelt down and washed his hands and face in the pool of salt water at the end of the chamber. Tossing a few branches on the fire the medicine man had built, he lay back on the soft bed of pine and balsam.

He wondered about traveling through time and whether other people had ever done it too. Just outside, Professor Pittfall should be camped in his tent—but he was not. If this place was an ancient Naugawump land, the professor hadn't even been born yet. Then how come Sam was alive and well?

Back home, did his folks know he had disappeared? Were his parents worried? Or—?

He groaned. There were just too many questions. Instead of trying to answer them all at once, he would stick to what he knew: He was caught in a twist of time. It was going to take some luck and some brains to get out of it. He would keep his eyes and ears open and sooner or later he would find a way back to the twentieth century.

The day hadn't been so bad after all, once he got over the shock of knowing what had happened to him. The Indians had been friendly, showing him around the village. After supper—mush again—the whole tribe had gathered around while Splashing Beaver spoke to them. They seemed very happy that Sam—Hobomock, they called him—had arrived.

"Splashing Beaver promised his people Hobomock will bring many days of good fishing," the medicine man later explained to him.

"Did you tell them where I came from?" Sam asked.

"From Temple of Keewaytin. That is where you come from."

"I mean, that you kidnapped me from another time?"

"They ask no questions," the medicine man declared fiercely. "You ask no questions. Here comes the princess. She talks to you now."

He marched away as the Indian girl approached. She smiled. "*Ahquay*, Hobomock."

Sam smiled back. "Hello."

A crown of red berries, taken from a holly tree,

was woven into her long black hair. She touched her chest. "Minnetonka."

He touched his chest. "Sam."

She pointed at him. "Hobomock."

"Sam," he muttered.

She pointed toward the setting sun. "Minnetonka."

He pointed across the water in the direction he thought Plymouth should be. "Burger King."

Puzzled, she pointed to the west once more and then to herself. "Minnetonka."

Sam caught on. She was named after the evening star shining above the horizon. Minnetonka, in the Naugawump language.

Thinking back later, he smiled to himself as he remembered what happened next.

"Burgaking?" she had asked, frowning.

"The hamburger god," he replied. "Listen, Princess, how about teaching me to speak Naugawump?"

They had sat on a rock by the sea for a long time and talked, using hand signals and drawing pictures in the sand with sticks. Somehow they had begun to make sense to each other. She had agreed to be his teacher and his guide.

Lying on his bed now, Sam repeated the few words he had learned that afternoon. Weeby, for eye. She had never before seen eyes that were nummanunk, the color of the sky. Her weebies were kotchanunk, like the oak leaf in autumn.

The fire in the Temple of Keewaytin was dying

out. The boy from Junction City, Kansas, couldn't keep his eyes open any longer. He pulled up the deerskin covering and fell asleep.

He greeted the princess the next morning with, *"Ahquay, kotchanunk weebies."*

Hello, brown eyes. It was his first real sentence in Naugawump.

She smiled. *"Ahquay,* Hobomock."

Sam spent many days with the Naugawumps. He wasn't sure of how many. He couldn't read Splashing Beaver's calendar, a big flat round stone with marks on it. His watch still said half past ten, so he kept it in his pocket and learned to tell time by the sun. One day Splashing Beaver squinted at his calendar and announced, *"Matterlawawa keeswush."*

Time to pick beans.

Sam had learned many words from Minnetonka simply by listening carefully as she talked and by asking questions. She showed him how to write Algonquin word-pictures. Each night, using a porcupine quill dipped in blueberry ink, he wrote down on bleached clamshells the words he had learned that day. He kept the shells in a basket and studied them later.

One hot afternoon when the bugs were biting pretty bad, the princess said, *"Micheenee keeswush."* Time of the everlasting flies. She had him rub animal fat on his body to keep the insects away. Messy, but it worked.

He often fixed his own meals, eating foods that he

79

would never touch at home, like succotash, fish and beans, and raw oysters. Sometimes he would dine with the Sachem and the princess. She would come for him in her canoe and take him across Tinkerton Sea.

She showed him something new almost every day. They visited the big sharpening rock where the men put cutting edges on spearheads and fish hooks. One of the older Naugawumps carved pipes out of soapstone. Dried pokeweed was their tobacco. Sam watched a canoe being made of pine saplings and birch bark, glued together with hot balsam sap. He watched the women grind corn with stone rolling pins. When he saw the field where the Indians grew corn and beans, he wanted to help weed but they wouldn't let him. He was not to do anything so lowly.

As Hobomock, he had to wear the feathered cape and keep his face painted. His main job was to help the fishermen. He did this each morning by standing on the temple roof and waving the numkonk at any canoe that came up to the shore.

"Namassack quay, Keewaytin!" he would call out.

Good fishing, Keewaytin!

The Naugawumps would then paddle out toward the ocean to look for lobsters, clams, codfish or whatever else they could catch. In the evening, while there was still light, they would stop by the temple on their way back to the village. They would climb to the roof and drop some of their catch down to Sam. It was their way of thanking Keewaytin.

"Numkonk quay-quay! Namassack quay! Ho-ho-ho, Hobomock!" they would shout.

The first time that happened, Sam was making his supper. He looked up to see what the fuss was about and a codfish landed on his head. He ducked as a large cohawg whistled by his ear. After that, he knew enough to stay out of the way.

Some things weren't easy for him, like cleaning his teeth with a corncob and lighting a fire with flint. But mostly life among the Naugawumps wasn't so bad. They tried to make him comfortable, probably because they thought he was bringing the fishermen good luck with the numkonk.

Sam never forgot for a moment, though, the fix he was in, wondering how he had gotten into it and how he would get out of it. Splashing Beaver would tell him nothing, but as he learned the Naugawump language, he was able to find out more and more things for himself. And finally the time came when he was told about what was going to happen to him.

He wasn't sure he would like it.

12. SPLASHING BEAVER'S PROMISE

THE DAY started out to be fun. Many more canoes than usual were gathered, carrying most of the men, women and children of the village. When Sam started to give the blessing, the people interrupted with cries of, *"Neetchy, Hobomock! Suqueeshy keeswush."*

Come along. It is suqueeshy time.

Puzzled because he had never before heard the word suqueeshy, Sam climbed into the canoe bearing the Sachem and the princess. *"Suqueeshy?"* he asked.

The princess laughed and wriggled her fingers but did not explain. Instead of heading out to the ocean as usual, the Naugawumps paddled to the shallow end of Tinkerton Sea. From his nearby canoe, Splashing Beaver pointed at Sam. "Bless *suqueeshy.*"

Standing up and waving the numkonk, Sam called out, *"Suqueeshy quay, Keewaytin!"*

With screams of excitement, most of the Indians jumped into the knee-deep water and stomped around in the mud, reaching down and pulling out wiggly black eels that they tossed into the canoes. Queppish, who remained in the boat while Minnetonka climbed out, jerked a thumb. *"Yuk-kee!"* he ordered.

Out.

Sam obeyed and a moment later he stood in the muck, feeling around with his feet in the ooze. Every so often something would squirm underfoot and he would reach down, grab it and toss it to Queppish. The princess was doing the same thing. He had caught four or five suqueeshies when the Sachem signaled that the hunt was over. At least a hundred eels had been caught.

While the other Naugawumps went back to the village with the catch, Queppish paddled Sam and the princess to the temple and left them there after seeing to it that she threw a suqueeshy down into the temple for the seafood god, Keewaytin. When Sam climbed down the ladder, he saw the eel slither into the salt-water pool and disappear. It could escape into Tinkerton Sea by way of the underground channel.

He and the princess sat on the edge of the pool and washed the mud off their feet. Talking in Naugawump language, she told him the suqueeshies would be sliced and fried on hot coals.

"Yum-yum," she smiled. Then her smile was gone and tears appeared in her weebies. When Sam asked why, she replied, "We eat *suqueeshy* at Keewaytin *pockatunk keeswush.*"

"Pockatunk?"

She traced the shape of a lobster in the dirt. Sam remembered that the god Keewaytin inhabited that form. He asked her why the thought of the pockatunk keeswush made her cry.

"Gutch hua—"

When the moon is full—

"Keewaytin sutkokish Hobomock—"

Keewaytin takes Hobomock away—

"Ouganit!"

Forever!

Hold on here, Sam thought. What's this all about? Back to the twentieth century? To lobster heaven? Little by little he got the whole story from her.

Fishing had been bad for the Naugawumps, she told him, for a whole year. The tribe blamed Splashing Beaver, who wore the sacred numkonk. Splashing Beaver blamed the fishermen, saying they were not offering enough of their catch to Keewaytin. But the less they caught, the less they wanted to throw into the temple for the seafood god.

The wise Sachem Queppish, however, declared that the fishing would get better when Keewaytin was made a gift of something special—an alive Hobomock. The medicine man must bring one by the first full moon after the suqueeshy keeswush, when Keewaytin would make his yearly visit to the temple. So Splashing Beaver, using his magic powder, sakopagunkum, had traveled through time searching for a Hobomock—until he came across Sam.

When the Naugawumps saw Sam, whose weebies were nummanunk and whose skin was wappinunk, the color of spring squash, they were pleased. He was something special all right. But was he a true Hobomock? Yes, for when he used the numkonk to bless the fishermen, they caught more fish. The tribe was very happy.

But the princess wasn't happy. She liked Sam and she didn't want anything to happen to him. What could happen? Well, at the full moon there would be a big festival at the temple. Keewaytin would appear and would be given the finest gift of all, a live Hobomock, to keep him content for another year.

Minnetonka pointed at Sam. "You are Hobomock."

The way she told it, the sacred lobster would show up in the pool inside the temple. After a feast and dancing, the Hobomock would have to go swimming with it. Sam knew that a lobster could really hurt a person with its powerful claws, one a cutter and the other a crusher.

But it was nothing to worry about. He figured that if he could somehow manage to be wearing his sneakers, he could get through the swim okay, without losing a finger or a toe. He could grab the creature by the back and hold it out, away from his body. He might even whittle a couple of little pegs, as lobstermen do in New England, and stick one behind each claw muscle to clamp it shut. It would be worth a try. And when the swim was finished, the Naugawumps would be pleased. With the festival a success, and with Keewaytin out of the way, Splashing Beaver could send Sam back to his own century.

"Minnetonka will miss Hobomock," the princess said.

"Cheer up, it can't be that bad," Sam replied. "Remember, *kuttenan tamook, nummet songash.*"

When a roof leaks, sunshine can enter.

It was a favorite saying of the Naugawumps when they wanted to look on the bright side of things. Sam was glad to see Minnetonka manage a little smile. "I'll miss you too," he said.

But he really felt pretty good about his chances of returning home. The next time he saw Splashing Beaver, he asked him about the pockatunk keeswush.

"It is a fine party," the medicine man told Sam. "You will have fun."

"What about the part where I get into the water with the lobster?"

"Oh, yes. Very important to make peace with Keewaytin. He will like Hobomock very much. Then Keewaytin will make good fishing for a long time."

"So my job will be finished. I won't have to bless the fishermen anymore and you can send me back to my own time."

The Naugawump paused for a moment, then replied, "Yes, if what you want."

"It is what I want. How soon does this shindig take place?"

"*Neetchy.*" He led Sam to the stone calendar next

to the temple wall, knelt down and studied its shadows and grooves. He held up four fingers. Sam grinned happily. In four days he'd be out of here and on his way home! He could take off the crazy cape and get back into comfortable dungarees and sneakers. It would be so good to see the professor and Miss Tinkerton again, to tell them all about his adventures with the Naugawumps, to have some of Diggins' wonderful meals and to flop into that big feather bed.

Sam looked into Splashing Beaver's painted face, which didn't show what he was thinking. Sam hoped he could trust the medicine man. He would have to.

13. THE SACRED LOBSTER

SPLASHING BEAVER was right. Sam did have a good time at the festival—for a while. The Naugawumps had started the preparations early in the morning, picking a spot behind the temple where they dug a pit, built a fire and put in a layer of rocks. One man stayed there and kept the blaze going with firewood.

Another place was cleared and swept under the direction of the medicine man, who was wearing his spooky mask, ankle and elbow feathers, and fancy painted designs on his arms and legs and chest. After the clearing was ready, he had his helpers arrange some stone seats in a half-circle, where the oldest and most important Naugawumps could be comfortable while eating and watching the show.

The women brought baskets and clay pots filled with food and drink. The medicine man waved his magic wand over everything to do away with the evil spirits that were supposed to be hiding there, hoping to spoil the party.

After the fire had been going for quite a while and the stones were red hot, the men threw wet seaweed on top of it, making clouds of steam rise into the air. Over the seaweed they dumped dozens of live lobsters and covered them with another layer of seaweed. Then they added food separated by layers of seaweed—clams, corn, sweet potatoes, white potatoes, sliced eels, bread, wild turkey legs and breasts, onions—until there was a big steaming mound, which they sealed by covering it with a straw mat.

Sam had a good view of the festival from the top of the temple. A seat had been put there for him and one each for Queppish and Minnetonka, who were wearing their finest clothing. Sam's face was painted in blueberry and cranberry colors and he was wearing the feathered cape and fancy leggins. To be ready for the big event with Keewaytin, he had put on sneakers instead of moccasins and he wore his dungarees underneath the loose-fitting Indian pants. The numkonk hung around his neck. In his pocket were the little wooden pegs he would use to lock the lobster's claws. He also had his rolled-up tee-shirt with him.

By the middle of the day, the whole tribe had arrived. They beached their canoes on the sand and gathered at the clearing. Some people sat on the stone seats, some on the ground. Others moved around busily, getting ready to take part in the ceremony. Cups of hot apple juice and oysters on the half shell were passed around. The mound continued to steam.

Splashing Beaver began the party by performing a dance and singing his *"Neeshun keesuquit, kuhtah peyaum."* It was a message to Keewaytin — and Sam was ready. He stood up and waved the numkonk. The tribe chanted in response.

After that, when everyone had settled down again, a group of young people put on a short play, acting out the history of the tribe. Sam understood some of it but the princess had to explain the rest of it to him. It was supposed to show how the earth was first created and how the Naugawumps came to be on it.

Then came the dances. They went on and on. When dancers grew tired, others took their places. The dances had a meaning to the Indians but Sam lost interest. He swallowed some raw oysters and washed the tasty treat down with cider. As the day wore on, he thought the drink was making him drowsy. He noticed that some of the Naugawumps had become more boisterous than usual and he wondered if the cider was the reason or if it was just due to the excitement of the festival.

When the moment finally came to open the steaming mound, he was happy. Like the others, he was hungry. People pounced on the food, digging it out of the seaweed and passing it back through the crowd to friends or taking it for themselves. They howled, half in joy and half in pain, as the hot food and seaweed burned their fingers. When they reached the bottom layer, there were the bright-red cooked lobsters — enough for everyone.

One of the women brought Sam and his two

companions their food. Sam had already learned from Minnetonka how to crack open the lobster claws with a stone, suck out the juice and then pick out the meat with a sharpened bone hook. It was delicious and so were the potatoes and corn. Now the sounds of the drums, the chanting and dancing were gone. Instead, the only sounds were the munching and the smacking of lips that go with a fine feast. It was the first time since arriving in Naugawump country that Sam had seen so much good food at one time.

He chewed on a wild turkey leg. *"Quay-quay."*

Very good.

Minnetonka nodded in agreement. She was breaking open a lobster tail to get at the meat inside.

"How can you cook and eat pockatunk if it is sacred?" Sam asked her.

"Only Keewaytin is sacred. Other pockatunks are to be eaten," she replied, glancing over her shoulder at the full moon coming up over the horizon. In the west, the sun was setting. The time was near.

Without thinking, Sam put his hand on the numkonk and was startled to hear a great roar from below. The tribe had surrounded the temple. All the people were staring up at him, crowding as close to the walls of the temple as they could, singing and waving their arms.

"Pockatunk Keewaytin! Utch kukketaff ktamonk!"

Splashing Beaver came out of the crowd, climbed the steps and peered down through the entrance into the temple chamber. Queppish and Minnetonka fell to their knees and stared into the opening too.

"*Keewaytin neetchy!*" the princess exclaimed.

Keewaytin comes.

"*Yukkee, Hobomock, yukkee,*" the Sachem said.

He was ordering Sam into the temple.

The medicine man turned to Sam. "Give back sacred cape. Keewaytin does not eat feathers."

Wondering, Sam took off the cape and handed it over. The medicine man reached out. "Now numkonk."

As Sam obeyed, the princess tried to stop him, crying out, "No! *Quittianit quay munatch!*"

You need it for good luck, she was telling him.

Quickly the Sachem grabbed his daughter and held her back while Splashing Beaver took the numkonk from Sam's neck. Angrily he repeated the Sachem's order. "*Yukkee, Hobomock.*"

Sam stood at the entrance and looked down. In the dusk there was just enough light for him to notice a surprising change—the temple floor was flooded! The full moon had caused a high tide to come in through the underground channel. Everything—including Sam's bed—was floating. But where was Keewaytin, the sacred lobster? Sam leaned over and looked more closely. No point in just jumping in before setting eyes on the little fellow. Suddenly a hand in the small of his back shoved him and he went flying into the gloom, landing in the water on his hands and knees with a great splash. He quickly stood up.

"Sho-sho, Hobomock," he heard Minnetonka say. Farewell.

But there was no time for farewells or for finding out who had pushed him. Sam was standing in ankle-deep water and a hungry lobster was on the loose. An empty basket floated nearby. He picked it up. He took a tomahawk from a shelf and got ready for action, backing away from the other end of the chamber where the water would be about four or five feet deep in such a high tide.

The Naugawumps were singing loudly. Many of them were jammed together at the window openings, trying to see what was going on inside the temple. Sam peered into the gloom. There! A ripple in the water. An object moved toward him. Good thing he had his sneakers on. He held out the basket as the lobster came closer. It reached the basket. The plan was working. Scoop it up and everything would all be over. But just as Sam was about to do that, he felt a lash across his shoulders. Turning, he raised his tomahawk and struck out at a whip that was slashing back and forth. It was wet and slippery. Suddenly there was another whip, about the thickness of a garden hose. The slimy things swayed here and there, brushing up and down his body.

Sam turned around to face the lobster again. But instead of gliding into the basket, it raised itself up, water glistening on its green-blue surfaces. And the frightening truth was now told: What Sam saw was not the whole lobster, it was only a claw! And the

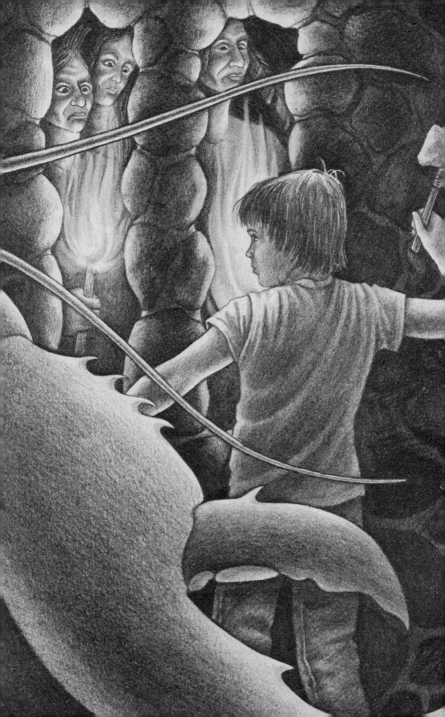

claw was big—as big as the spare tire on Professor Pittfall's safari wagon.

As Sam watched in horror, the huge claw crashed down on the basket, smashing it and splashing water all over. Then the other tremendous claw swished through the air and smacked the water. Sam took a step backward and felt the whips touch him again. No, they weren't whips, they were gigantic feelers!

He whacked at the nearest claw with the tomahawk. It was like hitting a stone wall. The weapon bounced off the shell, causing the shock to run up and down his arm like a jolt of electricity. When he dropped the tomahawk, the claw snapped its handle into bits.

Now, from the deepest part of the pool, two bulging, purplish eyes approached. They were the size of basketballs and beneath them great hairy jaws opened wide enough to swallow Sam. Behind these the shiny back rose up like a submarine surfacing. Sam's heart practically jumped out of his mouth.

Keewaytin, the sacred lobster of the Naugawumps, was a monster!

14. ESCAPE

SAM'S KNEES shook, the way they did one day when the bull chased him on the farm. Scared as he had been then, he had been able to run to the fence and climb over it safely. But here there was no fence, no way out except the way he had come in. And no help was coming from that direction. Queppish and Splashing Beaver watched gleefully, while Minnetonka cried.

The rest of the tribe was shouting through the windows and from what Sam could understand, they were cheering for the lobster. "Go gettum, Keewaytin!" they seemed to be saying.

The giant feelers slapped at him. The great claws reached out for him. One of those could cut him in two. Along the edge of the jaws there were short, shovellike legs that wiggled back and forth, waiting to scoop food into the slimy mouth. The sound they made was like a hundred people sucking through a hundred straws in a hundred empty soda glasses. Then the claws beat the water in a frenzy. Behind the huge body, the great tail flapped up and down.

Keewaytin was climbing out of the pool and into the shallow water to catch this juicy Hobomock— Sam Churchill—that had been sent for pockatunk keeswush.

Whenever Sam backed against the wall, the Indians at the windows shoved him forward. He looked around for a weapon—anything—but it was hopeless. Then he heard Minnetonka wish him good luck.

"Quay munatch, Hobomock."

He looked up in time to catch the numkonk she dropped to him before anyone could stop her. The medicine man shouted angrily at the princess. *"Googlush!"* Fool! Then he said to Sam, "Return it now."

Sam held the leather thong. Nice of Minnetonka to try to help, but a machine gun would have been more useful. Then he noticed that the lobster had stopped thrashing about. Its purplish eyes moved with the numkonk as Sam swung it back and forth. The claws barely quivered and the feelers collapsed. The sacred claw had hypnotized the monster. The great body was quiet now. When the people at the windows saw this, they pulled back, moaning and groaning and making frightened cries.

Overhead, the medicine man again demanded the return of the numkonk. Sam wondered if he could bargain—the sacred claw for a trip back to the twentieth century. He quickly decided the idea was silly. The Naugawumps wanted him for one reason only—as a meal for Keewaytin. So, swinging the numkonk back and forth, he slowly approached the

97

seafood god. What a giant! It must weigh a hundred pounds, he guessed. Only its ghoulish eyes moved now, staring at the sacred claw.

From outside, moonlight came through the windows and made the lobster shell glisten. The shell was probably slippery, Sam thought, but he had to take a chance. Putting the numkonk in his pocket, he jumped over Keewaytin's head and onto the hard surface of the lobster's back. He slid and landed in a sitting position. The monster didn't move. Sam took a deep breath and slipped off into the deep water between the edge of the pool and the creature's body. If the underground channel was big enough to let this fellow in, it was big enough to let Sam out.

He kicked and paddled underwater, feeling his way through the tunnel by pulling and pushing against its rocky walls. When he thought he couldn't hold his breath any longer, his hands touched the end and he stood up, his head breaking the surface of the water. He gulped in fresh air and looked around. On the shore, only a few yards away, loomed the shape of the temple. It was surrounded by chanting Naugawumps. The Sachem, medicine man and princess were still on top, peering inside. None of them knew that Sam had escaped. They would figure it out soon enough and then it would be easy for them to find him standing there in the water.

What now? The canoes were farther down the beach. He might get away in one but he would never keep ahead of the powerful Naugawump paddlers. In the other direction the forest rose up, leading away from the shore of Tinkerton Sea and toward—what? He did not know. As he hesitated, he felt a rush of water on his ankles. It was coming from the tunnel. Keewaytin had awakened and was coming out after him! The monster would be flapping its tail in reverse, the fastest method of travel for a lobster. Just then Splashing Beaver shouted a warning to the tribe that Hobomock had gotten away. Everyone began to yell and run in circles.

Their confusion gave Sam a head start. He waded onto dry land and ran into the woods. Thank goodness for the gutch hua that gave enough light for him to see by. Behind him he could hear the angry tribe trying to get organized. For a while, at least, they wouldn't know which way he had gone.

He kept on, traveling up an easy slope until he came to a high spot where he decided it was safe to stop for a moment and look back. Now he couldn't see or hear his pursuers. That was when he remembered something Minnetonka had once told him. Indians don't like the night. They have no electric lights and in the darkness they can't see dangers such as wild animals, unseen traps and enemy warriors. Even though Sam didn't much like the dark himself, it made him feel safe. The Naugawumps probably wouldn't start after him until daybreak.

He hurried on through the forest of big oaks and dense pine trees. It was chilly but he couldn't stop now to do anything about his wet clothes. He wrung out his tee-shirt and put it on. That helped a little. Soon the ground leveled off. Somewhere around here, he guessed, was the spot where Tinkerton Manor would be built one day. If he was right, close by there was a hill with a lot of big rocks where he could hide.

After some searching, he found the place and, sure enough, tucked among three or four big boulders there was a cavelike hideaway. It didn't take long to shred some bark, light it with flint and get a fire going. The Indian leggins were drying; the deerskin shed water easily. He hung everything before the blaze.

Covering himself with pine needles and leaves, he lay down. No one would ever find him tonight. He dozed on and off. Between naps he threw wood on the fire and listened for Indians. He wasn't very tired. The run through the woods had been easy. And he certainly wasn't hungry after that clambake. His head was filled with thoughts of all that had happened to him, especially the attack by the giant lobster. Finally, as the fire warmed him, he fell sound asleep.

When Sam opened his eyes at dawn, it took him a few moments to remember where he was. When he did, he wasn't overjoyed. He was still a prisoner of time. Only Splashing Beaver could return him to his own century. But if he went back to the Naugawumps now, they would surely feed him to Keewaytin and this time there would be no mistake.

Was he doomed to spend the rest of his life in the

wilderness, running from Indian lobster-worshippers? He had better not hang around waiting for an answer. Get dressed and get going. And he was hungry again. The fire was almost out but the clothes were dry. He cleaned up and put on the soft and comfortable deerskin leggins. His watch still said half past ten. It was now August something-or-other, he figured. But what year?

Sam rolled up the watch and the numkonk inside his dungarees, tucked them under his arm and peeked out into the gray dawn light. The sky was filled with clouds. Good. Rain would hide his tracks. He scrambled up the boulders to the top of the rocky hill. Looking in the direction he had come from, he saw nothing stirring. He heard only the singing of the early birds. The Naugawumps were probably slow getting up after that festival of dancing, eating and singing.

Sam turned in the other direction. The land sloped down toward the large bay that was a part of the Atlantic Ocean. The sky was gray all around. There was little wind and the sea was calm. A long, narrow sandbar stretched out from the mainland. Like an arrow, it pointed to the middle of the bay, straight at something Sam never in the world expected to see: a funny-looking little square-rigged sailing vessel.

His heart thumped. Hadn't he seen that ship before? Or one just like it?

Wasn't that the *Mayflower?*

15. A NEW COLONY

SAM STUMBLED and slid down the rocky hill to the forest floor and ran toward the bay. As the trees thinned out, he stopped to take another look. The ship was still there, moving slowly. He hurried down to the water and ran along the beach. Then he noticed that the vessel's sails were limp. She had stopped moving and was dropping anchor. It was the *Mayflower* all right. A longboat was lowered from the side. Men climbed in and began to row. Farther down the long sandy beach stood a large boulder, the only landmark of its kind in sight. The longboat headed toward it.

Sam looked around for a settlement or a sign that white men had been here before. There was none. Chills ran up and down his spine. The Pilgrims were about to make their famous landing. Plymouth Colony was going to be right here. Now he knew the year he was in. 1620! He stood and watched in awe as the boat neared shore. History was happening before his very eyes.

Then the men stopped rowing. The man in the stern was pointing—at Sam. He shouted but Sam couldn't catch the words. The others turned around to look in his direction. Now they, too, seemed excited. The helmsman moved the tiller slightly, the men dug their oars into the water again and the boat moved directly toward him.

Startled, he yelled, "No! No!"

He went to the water's edge and pointed to his left, up the beach. "That way! See that rock?"

But the men didn't listen. They only rowed harder and the boat rushed shoreward, finally scrunching onto the sand at Sam's feet. The men jumped out—half a mile from Plymouth Rock. There were five of them. They dropped to their knees and prayed aloud, giving thanks for having arrived safely in the New World. Then they surrounded Sam while their leader, the helmsman, asked the obvious question.

"Where dost thou come from?"

Sam was speechless. The Pilgrims had missed the Rock and it was his fault. And now he was supposed to explain how he came to be here. It would be impossible. He tried to think of a story the men would understand or believe, but he couldn't. They waited impatiently until finally one of them said, "Mayhap he is one of those left behind last year by Captain Gosnold, the explorer who gave this place the names of Cape Cod and Massachusetts."

Sam nodded brightly. "Yes, that is true. I got lost."

The helmsman clapped him on the shoulder. "Well, lad, Gosnold was no gentleman to sail without thee. Welcome to our company. I am Captain Myles Standish."

Sam could hardly believe it. The captain was the only famous person, except for Professor Pittfall, whom he had ever met. "Samuel Churchill, at your service, sir," he replied. "You must be the Pilgrims."

"Indeed," Captain Standish said. "Departed Plymouth, England, sixty-five days since. We are here to found a colony in the name of His Majesty, James the First."

"I was wondering, Captain Standish," Sam said politely, "if it wouldn't be a good idea to tie up your boat over there. You could step onto that rock and then onto the ground just the way you're supposed to."

Captain Standish followed Sam's gaze. "Yon boulder? Steer a boat at it when all this fine sandy beach lies before me? Surely thou jest, lad."

"Thou speak and dress oddly," one of the Pilgrims remarked.

"I lived with the Indians," Sam said, "and wore their clothes and spoke their tongue." The answer didn't explain his sneakers and tee-shirt but it seemed to satisfy the men.

"Thou wilt be of great help to us," Captain Standish declared, "should we meet any savages whilst here. But now let us find a place to build our town."

He had been steering for the mouth of a river, he explained, and had changed course only when he spied Sam on the beach. Now he wanted to explore the river for it would provide fresh water, a harbor and a good place to bring passengers and supplies ashore. The men shouldered their muskets and started off. Sam was glad to go along. Now the Naugawumps would think twice before trying to get him and the numkonk back.

He studied his new friends. They were short, none of them as tall as his father, who was barely six feet. All of them were bearded and they wore felt hats over their long hair that came down below their ears. Each one had on a long woolen coat and their pants were tucked into their boot tops, except for Myles Standish. His coat was made of leather. As they trudged through the sand in the summer heat, they took off their topcoats, revealing faded long-sleeved shirts.

When they reached the river, it turned out to be more like a brook than a river but the Pilgrims were pleased. Using the longboat, they shuttled back and forth between ship and shore, never once stepping foot on the rock, which was not far from the entrance to the brook. Men brought tools for clearing away the trees and shrubs and building their shelters. The women came with food and utensils and prepared meals for everyone. Sam ate what he was offered because he was hungry, but it wasn't very good—dried beef and something hard called sea biscuit.

The women also did laundry. They heated water in kettles, rinsed the clothes in the brook and spread them out to dry in the rigging of the *Mayflower*. Since leaving England, this was their first chance to get really clean.

Sam learned that quite a few explorers had sailed up and down the New England coast in recent years. Some of them had kidnapped Indians and taken them back to Europe. Sometimes Indians had captured sailors who were never seen again. So his story didn't seem unusual to those who heard it. The Pilgrims had too much to do and to think about to ask him many questions. They were very tired from their long voyage and just wanted to get settled.

Everyone was glad to have Sam's help. It was one more hand for all the work to be done. Temporary homes had to be built for the twenty families. Including children and servants, there were about one hundred people in all. Even though it was raining now, they got right to work. Houses were made by filling wooden walls with mud and covering them over with a steep roof of branches and a thatch of thick marsh grass that was supposed to be waterproof. Farmers began to clear fields and plant corn and potatoes while hunters went into the woods to look for game. Sam hoped the sound of their guns would scare away the Indians.

He helped by carrying mud from the brook. By the end of the day, two houses were almost finished. Everyone returned to the ship to spend the night. Sam went with them, getting a strange feeling as he climbed aboard the real *Mayflower*, not the replica that he and Professor Pittfall had visited. The main difference was that this one was crowded. And it smelled musty below deck.

After a supper of stew made from rabbits the hunters had brought back, the Pilgrims gathered on deck for prayer, followed by short speeches. First Captain Standish spoke and then Governor Bradford. The captain told, for those who had not yet been there, of the work that had been done ashore and what the land was like. He read out the names of those who would work the next day and what their jobs would be.

When it was the turn of the governor, a gray-haired gentleman wearing a nice velvet jacket, he asked the Pilgrims to be patient just a little longer until their homes were built.

"Our hearts are much comforted," he added, "by the bravery and courage shown by our people while crossing the mighty ocean that separates us from England. It is therefore fitting that we give our settlement a name that will remind us of our link to our homeland."

Once again Sam had the thrill of seeing history in the making.

Governor Bradford turned and waved toward the land. "I hereby give our colony the name of Atlantic City."

"Hear! Hear!" cried the people, clapping their hands in approval.

"Atlantic City, Massachusetts!" several of them shouted, trying out the new name.

Sam couldn't believe his ears. First the Rock, and now this. The Pilgrims were supposed to make history, not change it. What could he do? He was no good at speaking in front of a crowd but this called for action. Pushing through to the front of the group, he nervously raised a hand for quiet.

Would they listen to him? He would have to speak their language.

"Stoppeth thyselves!" he shouted in what he thought sounded like Olde English.

The Pilgrims stared at him in wonder.

"Who art thou?" the governor demanded.

"This is the stripling left over by the Gosnold company," Captain Standish explained.

"Then he be daft from exposure," the governor said angrily. "Throw him in irons."

"Wait!" Sam cried. "Listeneth to me. The name of Atlantic City hath been taken. I mean, it will be taken. I have a much better idea."

"Not better than mine," the governor spluttered.

"Name thy colony in honor of the city in England to which you owe so much."

There was a moment of silence while everyone thought that over. Then someone called out, "New London?"

"How about Boston?" another voice cried.

"No," Sam said. "Plymouth, the seaport from whence you sailed for this new land."

There were murmurs from the people. "Plymouth. Plymouth, Massachusetts." They seemed to like the sound.

Captain Standish repeated it. "Plymouth? Why not? Verily a pretty name for a pretty town."

The governor scratched his beard and looked at his companions. Then he announced, "Plymouth it shall be."

The Pilgrims cheered. Sam breathed a sigh of relief.

16. AN ADVENTUROUS FRIEND

SAM WAS given a straw pallet. Like some of the other people, now that the rain had stopped, he spread it on the main deck rather than sleep below. With his head on his rolled-up dungarees, he watched the clouds move across the face of the full moon, the same moon that was shining on the Naugawumps just a couple of miles away. Did the Indians know that the Pilgrims had landed? Would they try to get back the numkonk? Would they attack Plymouth? Would Splashing Beaver ever be friendly enough to return him to his home?

There was nothing about any of this in the history books that Miss Tinkerton had given him. It probably wasn't important enough to be written down. But it was happening to him. And it would become history. Was it happening the way it was supposed to? Had he changed things? What if he had sat quietly and let the colonists call the place Atlantic City or Boston?

He still didn't have any answers when he awoke at dawn, shivering. But he had thought of something he could do to help the Pilgrims and to keep himself busy. Everyone was getting up, eager to start another day in the New World. Women washed at one end of the ship, men at the other. After a breakfast of boiled cornmeal mixed with raisins, he crowded into the longboat. On shore Captain Standish was supervising the building of a wooden stockade to fence in the colony.

"Welcome to Plymouth, lad," he said. "Lend a hand here, if thou wilt."

"Gladly, sir, but first let me tell you what I've been thinking."

Sam then explained that in the swamps and bay there was an abundance of clams, fish, lobsters and eels that could be added to the Pilgrims' not very large food supply. The Englishman grew interested when he heard this.

"We know nothing of these waters. Canst thou harvest these foods for us?"

"Certainly, Captain, with help."

"Good. Then I shall send someone along to aid thee." He looked around and signaled to a fellow nearby. "Young man, over here, please."

The boy, who appeared to be about Sam's age, approached. His sleeves were rolled up and his pants were dirt-caked. He had been digging post holes. When Captain Standish told him what he had in mind, the boy smiled. "I am glad to take part."

"Fine. Go along with Sam Churchill here. He knows what to do. What is thy name, lad?"

"John Tinkerton."

"Ah, Squire Tinkerton's boy. Good luck to you both, then."

Captain Standish walked away while Sam stood in a daze. In the midst of his own problems, he had forgotten about the Curse and what the name Tinkerton meant. Now here he was eye-to-eye with the person who was responsible for it all.

"So you're John Tinkerton," he said.

"Aye, that I am. Is it so hard to believe?"

"No. It's just—well, let's get started."

What could he say? *I'm from the twentieth century. Your great-great-great-great-granddaughter has told me all about you. You are going to kidnap and maybe murder someone and get your family kicked out of town.* Nonsense. There was no way to talk about time travel to anyone in 1620, when people didn't even have automobiles or electricity.

As the days went by, the two boys became friends. John quickly learned how to dig for clams in the mud flats, how to dredge for lobster and how to spear flounder. They regularly brought in baskets of seafood and Sam showed the Pilgrim women how to cook the fish as he had been taught by the Naugawumps.

Sam kept a careful eye on his companion, who was supposed to be a bad guy according to the Tinkerton Curse. He thought a few times about trying to change history. He had talked the Pilgrims out of the Atlantic City and Boston goof. What if he was able to stop John from committing the crime that was going to cause all the trouble? That would stop the Curse before it got started. But it already *had* happened, as he, the professor and Miss

111

Tinkerton well knew. The puzzle was too tough to figure out now.

Anyway, nothing John said or did indicated that he might be a future criminal. He was always cheerful, always willing to learn and always ready to try something new or different. There was the day he brought back their first catch of suqueeshies, for instance. When the women saw the basket of eels, they screamed and the men said they would never eat any such thing. Sam cleaned and sliced a couple of the fish, barbecued them and persuaded John to taste them in front of the people.

"Delicious," the Pilgrim youth announced, gobbling a few slices. Thus some of the Pilgrims, not all, came to eat suqueeshies.

Afterward, when they were alone, John confessed, "I liked it not at all but I pretended so."

"You're a good actor," Sam said. "You fooled me."

"Most of them are so afraid," John said of the Pilgrims. "They just want to hide here behind the stockade. I myself think it is a great adventure. I want to explore, to find out all about this new land."

They were sitting on the ground, sunning themselves outside the house where John and his parents lived. After about a week, half of the Pilgrims were sheltered on land while the others, including Sam, lived on the ship until permanent houses were ready. Now the carpenters were busy on the frame dwellings, anxious to get a lot of work finished before the cold weather arrived. Other people worked at tasks such as cutting firewood, making barrels, pottery, brooms and clothing. In the spring another ship was due, bringing more people and supplies, but in the meantime, folks had a winter to go through here in Plymouth.

"Don't be too hard on your people," Sam told John. "It's frightening to be in a wilderness."

"But it is not," John replied. "Thou hast told of the natives living here. It is home to them, not a wilderness. It could be home to us strangers too."

"I suppose you're right," Sam admitted.

"I want to go there."

"What? Where?"

"Into the forest, to see what it is like."

"Wait," Sam protested. "Captain Standish has given orders, no one outside the stockade except to hunt and fish and tend the fields. It is for your own safety."

"Are there wild animals in the forest?"

"A turkey here, a deer there. Nothing to worry about."

"Be the Indians dangerous?"

"I'm not sure. They were most friendly to me but—"

"And they fear the darkness, you told me."

"I believe so," Sam said.

"Then," John declared, "I shall venture out at night."

Sam laughed. "Don't be silly. You would get lost."

"Not if thou art my guide."

"Me? No, sirree."

"Why not? Afraid?"

"Certainly not. I've been out there a lot, and at night too."

"Well?" John was taunting him.

"We should ask the captain's permission."

"He will say no. What he knoweth not, hurteth him not. And we might gain knowledge that would be of benefit to our colony."

Sam thought about that. The Pilgrims kept behind the stockade as much as possible. To survive, they would have to move outside to learn more about Indians, weather, wildlife, plants and sea life. They could not be forever fearful and remain ignorant of such matters. Maybe it was up to Sam and John to set an example for them, to show them that the wilderness could be a friend, not an enemy.

Also, Sam was interested in his own survival too. He wanted to know what the Naugawumps had been up to since he left them. Why hadn't they come after him? Perhaps they had forgiven him and Splashing Beaver would be willing to light up that magic travel powder again.

"All right, John," he agreed. "Tomorrow night if the weather's clear."

17. AN AWFUL DISCOVERY

THE NEXT NIGHT was clear but there was no moon to light the way. As Sam and John walked along the beach in the dark, thousands of stars looked down upon them.

John had received permission from his parents to spend the night aboard the ship. Instead, he and Sam had hidden along the shore until everyone else had gone to sleep. Sam was trying to retrace his steps to the temple. It wasn't easy. When he turned inland, looking for the hill where he had spent the night in the cave, he could see nothing in the blackness of the forest. All he could do was to stumble up the slope, guessing which way to go, with John following close behind.

Gradually their vision got used to the dark and they were able to keep from bumping into tree trunks. Soon they could walk in a fairly straight line. When they came across some big rocks, Sam knew he was in the right spot.

"Come on." He led John from boulder to boulder until he found the entrance to the cave. "This is the place I told you about."

"What about the Indian temple?" John asked.

"That's a lot farther. It'll be hard to find."

"Lead the way or I shall go alone."

So Sam led. They went on up the slope to the level part and then downhill again, trying to keep from straying. But stray they did, because when they broke out of the woods at the water's edge, the temple wasn't in sight. Sam was not surprised; it would have been pure luck to come upon it in the dark. John was excited though.

"What is that yonder?" He pointed across the water.

Dim firelight flickered in the distance. "It's the village of the Naugawumps," Sam told him.

"Let us go there."

"You can't without a canoe. It's a long walk around the shoreline."

"This is a large body of water?"

"It is."

"Does it have a name?"

"Uh—not yet," Sam answered carefully.

"Well, then." John picked up a stone and threw it. When he heard it splash, he announced, "I christen thee Tinkerton Sea!"

"That's very nice," Sam said. "But don't make so much noise."

"Where can we find the temple?" John asked quietly.

"I don't know where we are. It's either to the right or to the left."

"What is inside it? Why didst thou run from it?"

Sam told as much of the story as he thought

would make sense to the young Englishman. It certainly sounded crazy—the man-eating lobster, the clambake, the dances. John was interested in the power of the numkonk. He wanted to see it but Sam had left it safe in Plymouth.

"The sacred claw made them bow down to thee?"

"Yes, it did. And they would like to have it back, and me with it."

John was silent for a minute. Then he asked, "Is it the truth? Thou hast such a strange manner of speech. Where art thou from?"

The fellow was smart to suspect something but was he smart enough for the whole story? Sam decided no—not yet anyway. "London town," he replied.

John seemed to be satisfied. Now he insisted upon searching for the temple again. They decided to turn right. After quite a long walk along the shore, Sam knew they had taken the wrong way. He was glad because he wasn't sure he wanted to investigate that place in the dark. Finally they came to a stream that Sam knew emptied out of Tinkerton Sea and probably into Cape Cod Bay. Because the stream was too wide and deep to cross, they walked along the bank.

They had missed the temple. There wasn't time to turn back and start out again. After about an hour of following the winding brook through the woods, they saw an opening ahead and were pleasantly surprised to come up against the Plymouth stockade. Quietly they sneaked around it and headed to the bay, where the sky was turning gray as a new day dawned.

The next few days were rainy. That was all right with Sam because it gave him a chance to make plans. Spying at night wasn't going to tell him much. Spying in the daytime was risky. And what if the Indians showed up at Plymouth, trying to be friendly? When they saw Sam, they would probably start trouble.

He still hadn't made up his mind what to do next when, one nice day, John pestered him to make another trip into the woods. Sam said not yet. The English boy didn't argue and became rather quiet for the rest of the day while they fished for flounder, using worms as bait. When they parted after supper, John was still in a sober mood.

The next morning, when Sam stepped ashore from the longboat, his friend wasn't there to greet him. Hoping John wasn't too angry to help with the clamming, Sam set out to find him but ran into his father instead, coming from the stockade.

"Good morrow, Squire Tinkerton," he said in greeting.

"The same to thee, Master Samuel. And where might John be?"

Sam quickly guessed the answer. Not wishing to lie, he gave a non-answer. "We wanted to get an early start, sir."

"Ah, I see. He slept on board ship. I do wish he had told us. His mother is worried."

Now Sam was worried too. The fellow must have

gone into the woods by himself. He was insane to try something like that. Why hadn't he returned? Sam pictured John in the hands of Splashing Beaver. It could be very bad for the young Englishman.

Sam carried his basket down to the beach. The tide was low. He walked toward the water and dropped to his knees, gathering up the soft-shelled mollusks that were buried a few inches under the muck. Then he heard his name called. It was John, waving to him from the shore. Sam sloshed through the mud to the dry sand.

"Where have you been?"

"To the Tinkerton Sea," John replied with a grin. "And I have seen much. I have seen Indians at last."

Sam looked at the torn shirt and the scratches on his friend's face. "Are you all right? Did they hurt you?"

"They did not know I was there. I was up a tree."

"Up a tree?"

"Sit down and I shall tell you what happened." He flopped onto the sand. "I am tired."

He had set out alone after dark. To keep from getting lost in the woods, he had followed the brook upstream back to Tinkerton Sea and walked along its shore, hoping to find the temple. When he stumbled into a pile of stones and dry seaweed, he decided he had come across the clambake pit Sam had told him about. And then he saw the temple. As he stood there planning his next move, he heard a sound. It was a human voice.

"Silently, I crept up the temple wall," John went

on. "I peeked over the edge of the opening. Down below there was a small fire. A painted Indian knelt before it, dressed in the fine cape thou hast worn."

"That may be good news," Sam said. "They've picked someone else to be Hobomock. It lets me off the hook. Was there a ladder?"

"No. There was no way she could get out."

"She?"

"Yes. She heard me and looked up. I saw an Indian maiden with a crown of red berries on her head. She was crying."

Sam jumped to his feet. "The princess!"

"Be calm, my friend. Let me tell thee the rest."

"Yes, yes, go on."

Sam listened with half an ear as John related how the arrival of an Indian by canoe had forced him to climb a tree to keep out of sight. Sam knew the Indian was Splashing Beaver. The medicine man had lit more fires and had sung magic words, both inside the temple and out, and the Indian maiden had seemed to beg for mercy. It wasn't until dawn that Splashing Beaver had gone away, giving John the chance to climb down the tree and run to Plymouth through the woods.

"This is awful!" Sam exclaimed. "They're going to hand her over to Keewaytin. John, she saved my life. Now it is my turn. I must rescue Minnetonka from the claws of the lobster giant."

18. THE MAGIC POWDER

IT DIDN'T TAKE John long to make up his mind. "A fine adventure. Let us go!"

"Hold your horses," Sam laughed. "We have to get ready. Minnetonka is safe until the next full moon. First we must get permission to leave town after dark. I don't want to have to sneak out as we did before."

"Impossible. The captain will not allow it."

"You'll see. I have an idea."

When they returned to the town, Sam made his request of Captain Standish. "John and I must capture some night crawlers, sir, to use as bait. And those big worms come out only in the dark."

The captain pondered for a moment. "I see. Well, lads, if it be for the good of the colony, then proceed. 'Tis dangerous out there. Be careful. We shall watch for thy safe return."

Back at the Tinkerton house, Sam changed into his dungarees.

"You see, John, now if anything goes wrong, we shall be missed and there's a chance we would be rescued. Here, you wear these deerskin leggins.

They are much better in the forest than those baggy woolens."

After a supper of corn chowder, they said farewell to the Tinkertons and set out in the dusk, carrying their equipment as though they would be digging for worms. Once out of sight of town, they hid their gear and headed into the woods.

Arriving on the hill above Tinkerton Sea, they waited for complete darkness before going on. Now that he knew exactly where they were, Sam had little trouble in finding the temple. There seemed to be no Naugawumps about. The two boys approached silently and slowly and peeked in through one of the little windows.

The princess was alone, seated on a straw mat and staring at a tiny fire.

"Come on," Sam said. They crawled up the steps to the roof, found the ladder, lowered it through the entrance and climbed down.

A surprised princess cried out, "Hobomock!"

"Ahquay," Sam replied. "This is my friend John. We come to rescue you."

Her kotchanunk weebies flashed angrily. "I need no rescue. I am the Hobomock now. Keewaytin will come for me at the next full moon."

"What doth she say?" John asked.

"She's proud to be sacrificed to the lobster. It's an honor."

"If that be true, she is daft."

"Does Minnetonka really wish this?" Sam asked her. "To be crushed in the monster's claws?"

The corners of her mouth turned down and she

burst into tears. "No," she sobbed, "but it will make the shellfish god happy and bring good luck to my people. Minnetonka must obey Splashing Beaver."

"What does Sachem Queppish say?"

"Father is very ill. He is old. And I must be sacrificed for helping you to get away, for giving you the numkonk."

Sam translated for John.

"Tell her that the Pilgrims will care for her," the English lad said.

Gradually they calmed her and finally she removed the feathered cape and agreed to let them take her to Plymouth. She knew about the arrival of the Pilgrims and that Sam had gone to live with them after escaping from Keewaytin. "The historian has watched the foreigners," she told them.

"The historian?" Sam asked.

"The Naugawump who writes down all that happens to our tribe," she explained. "Here, I show you."

She went to a dark corner of the temple and returned with a clay tablet like those laid out on the library table at Tinkerton Manor.

"Well, I'll be darned," Sam murmured.

"There are many of these," she said.

Sam smiled. "Yes, I know."

"They tell us who and what went before, and when," she explained.

When John heard that the Indians had been spying on the Pilgrims, he was worried. "Will they try to harm us?"

124

The Naugawumps were very upset, she reported, at losing the numkonk. As soon as Queppish felt better, he would lead an attack on Plymouth to retrieve the sacred claw. And if the Pilgrims gave Minnetonka safety, that would be even greater reason for an attack. Splashing Beaver must get her back or he would have to go to all the trouble of finding another Hobomock. The Hobomock had to be of royal blood like herself or someone special like Sam, brought from another world.

Sam's ears perked up. "Will Splashing Beaver travel to another world himself?"

She nodded. "He does so when he wishes."

"How?"

"*Sakopagunkum.*"

"Sako—I've heard that word before." Sam remembered it as a part of the medicine man's yell when he threw the powder into the flames, sending Sam through time. What were the exact magic words? He asked the princess if she knew. She went again to the dark corner and this time she brought back a small leather pouch closed with a drawstring.

"This is secret. Only Splashing Beaver knows."

Sam held the little bag for a moment, then loosened the drawstring. The princess stepped back, frightened. Inside he found a soft, sandy substance and a big cohawg shell. Taking out the shell, Sam saw there was Naugawump writing on it. Only two words.

One of the words was sakopagunkum, which he translated as "spooky dust." The other word was strange to him, not like any Naugawump word he had ever learned. He tried to show it to Minnetonka but she hid her eyes and would not look. As far as he could tell, the word was pqtchx. Now he recalled that the medicine man had followed the shout of *"Sakopagunkum!"* with a peculiar sound. This must be it. Pqtchx.

Sam was excited. He had the powder and the magic words and he was in the right place. Maybe he didn't need Splashing Beaver in order to travel back—or ahead, he meant—to the twentieth century. It was worth a try. Now or never.

John had been watching with curiosity and impatience. "What is it?"

Sam grabbed his friend's arm. "I can't explain now. Listen, you must take Minnetonka outside. Wait for me and—this is going to sound strange—if I disappear, you take her back to Plymouth as fast as you can. Even without me. Understand?"

"I understand, but why?"

Sam pushed his friends toward the ladder. "Don't ask questions. Just do it."

The princess went first. *"Sho-sho,"* he said to her. Good-bye.

Sam held the young Englishman back for just a second. "You're a good and loyal friend, John. I shall never forget you."

"We shall wait for thee outside."

Alone now, Sam threw a few twigs on the fire and stared at the flames. What next? What are the right thoughts for time travel? He tried to remember more details about the only other such trip he had made but they were vague in his mind. Just get started, then. Try to relax.

Reaching into the pouch, he took out a small handful of powder. His fingers tingled as he touched it. Electricity? Nuclear energy? Slowly he sprinkled it on the fire. There was a poof! as a cloud of smoke arose. He felt the fumes enter his nose, eyes and lungs. He coughed. Now for the magic words! His eyes watered. He could hardly read the clamshell.

"Sakopagunkum!" he yelled.

He studied the other word. Pqtchx. He tried to say it aloud. His tongue squeezed against his teeth. His lips popped. His cheeks puffed. But no word came out of his mouth. Just a funny sputter. He tried again and again. He couldn't say it. And now it was too late. The puff of smoke floated up through the hole in the roof.

What went wrong? Did he really need a medicine man to cast the spell? He put his hands in his pockets as he asked these questions. He touched the numkonk and then a warm, sleepy sensation ran through his body from head to toe. Maybe its magic would make a difference. He hung it around his neck, kept one hand on it, looked at the writing on the clamshell and said, clear as a bell,

"Pqtchx."

He could say it now. He should have known. The numkonk was all-powerful. But the magic smoke was gone. Quickly he grabbed a handful of powder from the pouch and got ready to try again. Here goes! He threw the powder into the flames. There was a small explosion and a big cloud of smoke filled the temple. Once again his eyes filled with tears and he coughed but he managed to cry out, *"Sakopagunkum!"* He touched the numkonk and was ready to say the second magic word but before he could utter it, there was a hoarse cry at one of the windows. John's face appeared.

"Sam! Indians in canoes! Get out! We shall meet thee in Plymouth. Hurry!"

19. A CANOE RACE

SAM RUSHED to the window. John and the princess had already disappeared into the night, running into the woods. He dashed to another opening from which he could see Tinkerton Sea. Torches were blazing and their lights reflected in the water. At least two canoes were approaching the temple.

It was too late for the magic word. The cloud of smoke had thinned out. The spell was broken and now he had the problem of how to get away from the Naugawumps. If he were captured again, it would be the end of him. For a disguise he threw the feathered cape over his shoulders and then felt his way up the ladder. The Indians were just climbing out of the canoes. Sam slipped down the far side of the building and crouched, waiting to make a run for it. He thought about going down to the beach to draw the pursuers' attention away from John and the princess. The trouble with that plan was that three Naugawumps were loitering around a canoe there.

The other Indian had reached the temple roof and upon seeing the ladder there and discovering the princess missing, he yelled, *"Minnetonka yukkee!"* It was Splashing Beaver's voice. When his companions started toward the temple, Sam tried to dash down the beach but they spotted him and blocked the way. Two canoes were drawn up on the sand. Quickly, he pushed one of them away, jumped in the other one and shoved off. The Indians were right at his heels.

"There she goes!" one shouted in Naugawump.

"Minnetonka, neetchy-neetchy," called the medicine man, ordering Sam to come back, thinking he was the princess.

But when Sam threw off the cape and grabbed a paddle, he was recognized. "Traitor!" shouted Splashing Beaver.

Sam knelt in the center of the craft and dug the paddle into the water. The canoe shot forward, out into the darkness of the sea. Behind him the Indians were splashing in the water, going after the lost canoe. Sam swung to the right and headed for the town brook. If he could get there ahead of them, he might be safe.

Now the Naugawumps had the other canoe. All four of them crowded into it, two men doing the paddling, Splashing Beaver and the fourth man holding the torches. They made quite a bit of noise, which surprised Sam. He had always thought of Indians as being quiet people.

"Goomba! Goomba!" they yelled. Faster, faster.

The medicine man shouted insults at Sam in English. "Come back, thieving foreigner!" He was very angry.

130

The Indians were excellent paddlers, sending the boat through the water rapidly and on a straight course. They grunted with each powerful stroke so that even if Sam couldn't see them, he could hear them. Although they had a heavier load and he had a head start, they would soon catch up with him. He wished he could get rid of the musty sakopagunkum smoke that still stung his nostrils. He had swallowed a good lungful of it before he escaped from the temple.

Despite the dizzy feeling, Sam kept up the long, strong strokes, first one side and then the other, trying to keep the canoe going in a straight line. Where was that confounded brook? It had seemed so close when he and John had walked to it the other night. He paddled closer to shore so he wouldn't miss it in the dark. Then, looking over his shoulder, he saw that the Indians had stopped following him. Suddenly he knew why when his paddle struck bottom. He was on a sandbar! Now the Naugawumps were passing him and would cut him off up ahead. His canoe barely moved as it scrunched against the mud and sand.

Sam jumped out and began to walk, pulling the boat behind him. It was like going through soft cement. His legs felt heavier and heavier. He leaned forward, pulling, pulling, the soft sand holding his feet with every step he tried to take.

Ahead, the torches lit the spot where the Naugawumps awaited him in deep water at the end of the sandbar. He looked shoreward. There seemed to be a break in the length of the beach. It could be the entrance of the brook leading back to the Pilgrim colony. He went toward it. Soon the sandy bottom turned hard and the water was up to his waist. He had crossed the bar. Scrambling into the canoe, he paddled a short distance and, sure enough, entered the town brook.

Now the Indians saw him. *"Goomba-goomba!"*

His lungs wheezing, his arms aching, Sam paddled furiously, following the current the best he could in the dark. The forest closed in on both sides. Branches brushed against his face. He felt safer now, knowing the trees were guarding him. He heard no cries from his pursuers and saw no torches. Had they given up? Were they afraid of entering the woods at night? He hoped so, but taking no chances, he kept on and on as fast as he could go through the black of the night until he slumped down, exhausted. He just couldn't lift the paddle one more time.

But the Naugawumps had abandoned the chase. And Minnetonka had been saved. The venture had been a success. Now he felt like sleeping. His head ached and he was drowsy. Sam closed his eyes and let the canoe drift toward Plymouth — and safety.

Everything was so quiet. The loudest sound was the thumping of his heart. The craft bumped against the shore, startling him. He pushed it off into the stream again. Gosh, it was dark! All the pilgrims would be in bed, unless John and Minnetonka had awakened them. Was there a light ahead? Yes, there was a fire alongside the stream.

As he came closer, he saw figures around the blaze. He couldn't believe it—they were Indians. But they weren't moving. They seemed to be frozen, like statues. Then suddenly one of them turned to look at Sam. It was Splashing Beaver!

How did he get there? Sam took hold of the paddle and tried to speed past but the medicine man let out a great cry.

"Boy! Bring back the numkonk! Return it to our tribe. Splashing Beaver speaks."

The Naugawump leaped into the water and grabbed the end of the canoe. Sam lifted the paddle and brought it down with a loud slap on the side of the Indian's head, causing him to let go. The canoe rocked. Sam almost fell out. Splashing Beaver started after him again. Sam took the sacred claw from around his neck and threw it.

"Here, take your numkonk. *Pqtchx!*"

There was a blinding flash of light, then darkness and silence. Dazed, Sam dug his paddle into the water and sent the canoe ahead, around a bend in the stream. When he looked back, he couldn't see the fire or the Indians. A few moments later he came out into the sunshine, blinking his eyes.

On the shore he saw a group of tourists. They were wearing shorts and sandals and carrying cameras and handbags. A gray-bearded man in breeches grabbed the canoe and tied it to the dock.

"Enjoy yourself, sonny?" he asked with a toothless grin.

Sam was in the twentieth century again!

20. THE RETURN

KNEES SHAKING, Sam climbed out of the canoe. Bewildered, he looked back into the gloomy Tunnel to Yesterday. It had become a tunnel to today! He hadn't been ready for such a quick change. Somehow the magic powder and words had done their job. He took out his watch. The sweep hand was moving. It had started telling twentieth-century time again. He strapped it onto his wrist. Home again! A wonderful feeling. He let out a whoop of joyous laughter.

The gray-beard frowned. "Was it funny, then?"

"The night crawlers," Sam said with a grin. "I didn't take the night crawlers back to Captain Standish."

The old man said, "All right, sonny, just move along. Make room for the others."

Sam was glad to. He hurried out of the gate and turned right, heading in the direction of Tinkerton Manor. He had to get back to Queppish Hill in a hurry. There was much ·to do and much to tell Professor Pittfall and Miss Tinkerton. He held out his thumb at the cars coming toward him. This road, he remembered, connected with the Sandwich road that passed Tinkerton Manor. A family in a Studebaker sedan stopped for him and he was running up the manor driveway ten minutes later.

Without stopping at the house, he kept going across the meadow and into the woods. How strange! Just last night—three centuries ago—he was walking on this very ground. And now he saw Tinkerton Sea ahead—but there was a difference. Instead of a Naugawump village, he saw a yacht club. Sailboats instead of canoes.

At Queppish Hill he found Professor Pittfall puffing on his pipe and hovering over the table of relics, pencil and notebook in hand. It was good to see the big guy again.

"Hi, Professor!" he called out.

The explorer turned. "Samuel, my boy, where have you been? Did you bring my lunch?"

"Lunch?"

"Why, yes. Although I had morning tea and crumpets, I do have a sense of starvation right now. Well, let's hope Elvira shows up soon." He pointed his pencil at the table. "Here's bad news, Sam. They've stolen some more of our precious artifacts."

"Yes, I know."

"You know? You weren't here when I checked them this morning. How did you know?"

Now Sam had to remind himself of something. His adventures in 1620 had lasted for several weeks but as far as the professor was concerned, only one

135

night had passed. He shifted his memory back to the beginning of his trip through time and said, "You slept through all the excitement last night, Professor."

Pittfall was puzzled. "Excitement? What excitement?"

"I was yelling for you when I chased the thief."

"You chased the thief?"

"Yes. It was Splashing Beaver, the Naugawump."

"Splashing Beaver?"

"Yes. I caught him inside the temple."

"The temple? What temple?"

"That temple. Queppish Hill is a temple. Was a temple, I mean. Come on, I'll show you something."

Sam climbed the hill and cranked the big fellow to the top with the windlass. He then descended the ladder and again found himself inside the mysterious shrine where so many unbelievable events had taken place. The chamber was damp. He shivered. Around the walls the stolen objects were still where the Indian had put them.

"Lower the basket, please," he called.

One by one he sent the artifacts up. After about an hour's work, he and the professor had them all arranged on the table again. The explorer had spoken very little. Now, after he had checked every item against his list and found them all there, he turned to his assistant.

"Why did you do it, Samuel?"

"Do it?"

"Sneak all these things back inside Queppish Hill,

I mean. Letting me believe they had been stolen."

Sam's jaw dropped. The blood rose to his face. He gulped and was almost speechless. Finally he mumbled, "Splashing Beaver."

"Yes, the Naugawump. You mentioned him. You said you caught him. Where is he now?"

"He—we went—I just saw him—in the Tunnel to Yesterday—"

"Made out of wax, right? And he came here last night and put our finds back inside the hill?"

Sam slumped onto a stool. The thought flashed through his head—no one would ever believe what had happened to him.

The professor put a hand on his shoulder. "I've heard about your sense of humor," he said with a smile. "Let's just say this is one practical joke that didn't work. Okay?"

"Okay," the boy answered weakly.

"Now we can get on with Miss Tinkerton's business. And here she comes now. She has brought sustenance, I hope."

The limousine jounced into view with Diggins at the wheel. He parked just behind the safari wagon. The lady hopped out, carrying a picnic basket. The archeologist was happy. "My dear Elvira, what a pleasure to see you!" He was looking at the basket when he said it.

Now Sam realized he was hungry too, not having eaten since 1620. That should have been funny but he had too much on his mind to laugh. He had learned so much of the past about Queppish Hill and about Miss Tinkerton's ancestor, John. How could he pass this knowledge along to his friends? Tell them he was there when it all happened? Fat chance they would swallow that line. He was going to have to think of something that would make sense to them.

"Isn't that right, Sam?" a voice asked.

"Wha — I'm sorry, Miss Tinkerton. I was day-dreaming, I guess."

"I told Potter that to make up for your foolishness, you would simply work harder."

"Yes, ma'am. Of course I will."

He was lucky. They were being very nice to him. That didn't solve his problem, though, and the rest of the day he thought about it while he worked inside the temple. He collected several more Naugawump relics — knives, pottery, another mask or two — and sent them up to the professor.

The temple had changed only a little in more than three hundred years. Now it was covered with soil and sand so that a person couldn't look through the window openings. And the pool, where Keewaytin had attacked him, was almost all filled in with dirt. He found himself wondering about John and Minnetonka. Were they safe? Hold it! He gave his face a little slap. They were — they had to be dead and gone.

When the day's work was done, he climbed the ladder in a daze, glad to get out of the chamber. It wasn't a place where a person could think straight. And there was always the scary chance that the medicine man might make an appearance again.

"Well, Sam," the professor said as they rode Lulu

back to the manor house, "tonight we don't have to sleep in the tent and watch for thieves, do we?"

Dinner that evening tasted better than Sam had ever known it to. "The Pilgrims and the Indians don't eat this well," he declared. "I mean—didn't eat this well."

"Most people around the world don't eat like this," Professor Pittfall said. "They are starving, or close to it."

Now Sam felt guilty about stuffing himself but since he didn't wish to be impolite, he ate everything that was offered him. When they went into the library, where Diggins served coffee to the grown-ups, he wandered about the room, reading the titles of books and finally stopping at the long table where the hundred and twenty-one clay tablets were still spread out.

He picked one up and glanced at the tiny hieroglyphics. The first line seemed familiar to him. *When the groundhog sleeps,* it read in Naugawump language. He looked at another sentence. *"Squanamock keeswush,"* he said aloud. "Time to weed cornfield."

Professor Pittfall looked at him. "What did you say?"

Sam froze. He could read the Naugawump writing! Even the professor had not been able to. How could he ever explain it to them? He faked a yawn. "I said it was time I went to my comfortable bed."

He said good night and went upstairs. The soft

139

mattress was comfortable all right, a lot better than pine needles or a straw mat. But he didn't sleep right away. His mind was too busy with the Naugawump hieroglyphics. From what he had just seen, those tablets told about the events in the life of the tribe. They were the history records Minnetonka had told him about. And some of the tablets might describe what had taken place after he escaped from Splashing Beaver. If he could only remember all that the princess had taught him about the language!

Suddenly it came to him. The dictionary. He had written it himself on clamshells. The shells could still be in the temple, in that corner where he had tucked away each one as he finished it.

Sam fell asleep full of hope. Tomorrow he would find the clamshell dictionary.

21. THE TABLETS TALK

BUT THE SHELLS weren't there. Sam spent much of the morning poking into the darkest corners of the temple, using the searchlight and a hand-trowel, scraping and digging. He found a knife and a tomahawk but not the shells on which he had translated the words of the Naugawump language into English. He turned over the new objects to the professor, saying, "I was hoping to find clamshells."

"We don't need clamshells," Pittfall said. "We need information about the Tinkerton Curse. That's the reason we are here and so far we have found nothing."

Sam was still hopeful. "Maybe today's the day."

"Besides," the professor added, "Indians wouldn't save clamshells. That's why you don't find any."

Of course! Since the shells meant nothing to the Naugawumps, they had thrown them out. The clamshell pages of his dictionary were probably scattered somewhere under the pile of dirt and sand that covered and surrounded Queppish Hill. But where? He couldn't dig up the entire place. Then the thought came to him: There was a way to find objects that were underground.

"Professor, Pittfall," he asked, "wouldn't the dowsing rod tell me where certain clamshells are buried?"

The big fellow looked up from his work. "You were successful once before, weren't you? Try it again, although I fail to understand this sudden interest in clamshells."

Sam went to work right away, using the V-shaped twig with which he had discovered the entrance to the temple. He gripped the ends of the rod in his upturned palms and walked to the foot of Queppish Hill. He stood there for several minutes with half-closed eyes, forgetting everything but the important message he wanted to pass through the single end of the divining stick.

Then he started to make a slow circle of the hill. The end of the rod was pointing straight ahead of him, waist-high. He shut out all unimportant sights and sounds. Through his mind, over and over, ran the words, *Clamshell pages, speak to me.* He held the twig gently as he walked carefully along one side of the dirt-covered temple wall. He passed the trench he had first dug into the hillside.

"I am waiting," he whispered, "for Mother Earth to send me a message."

Sam's eyes were open just enough to keep him from stumbling. His mind was as in a dream. Suddenly, as he turned toward the side of the hill nearest Tinkerton Sea, he felt a tug. The pampong twig twisted in his hands and turned down slightly. He took one more step forward and it was aiming at his toes.

142

It took only a minute to get the spade and dig up a clamshell. With shaking hands, he turned to the bleached inside and saw the words he had once painted there with a porcupine quill dipped in blueberry ink.

Colors

NUMMANUNK — sky blue
KOTCHANUNK — oak leaf brown
WAPPINUNK — squash yellow

"Professor, come quickly," he called, turning another spadeful of dirt and uncovering a shell that listed the keeswush holidays.

The archeologist examined the two shells. "Bless my booties, Samuel! I do believe you have made a momentous discovery. Dig on, my boy, dig on."

Grinning happily, Sam dug on, turning up more and more pages of his clamshell dictionary. He rested briefly when Miss Tinkerton showed up with lunch.

"Thank goodness you remembered the lemonade, Elvira," said the professor, taking a large glass of it. "I've worked up quite a thirst on this hot day while watching Sam."

Sam smiled and bit into his junior club sandwich, listening to the professor explain the new discovery to her. She studied the shells. "I wonder when these were written and by whom."

"If they help us read the Naugawump tablets found in the stone chamber," the professor declared, "we shall find out something about your ancestor, John Tinkerton, I daresay."

Sam picked up his spade. I daresay too, he thought. He could hardly wait.

That evening after dinner they began. The hundred and twenty-one clay tablets covered the library table and so the clamshell dictionary had to be spread on the floor, on chair seats and elsewhere around the big room. Matching them with the tablets and finding the meanings of the words was quite a task, especially for the professor. But as Sam looked at the words, the Naugawump language came back to him so that he was able to read many of the historian's tablets.

When the clock struck ten, they had translated only two of the tablets. They told about a bad winter when the bay had frozen over. Professor Pittfall yawned. "It's late. Let's finish this tomorrow."

"I'd like to work at it a bit longer," Sam said.

"Okay. You seem to be pretty good at it. But don't stay up too late. Good night."

"Good night, Professor. Good-night, Miss Tinkerton."

He did stay up late. First he arranged the clamshell dictionary by subjects such as food, seasons and religion. Then he found the tablets that were written in 1620. Once he was organized, everything went smoothly. He was reading the history tablets as he would a newspaper and learning some surprising things.

The next morning Miss Tinkerton exclaimed,

"Don't tell me you stayed up all night. Your mother wouldn't like that."

"I couldn't sleep. I've found out a lot."

He talked while the professor ate his eggs and sausage. "Queppish Hill was a temple where the Naugawumps worshipped their seafood god, Keewaytin. He was a gigantic man-eating lobster. A funny thing happened there around the time the Pilgrims landed. John Tinkerton had a part in it."

"You mean you have found out something about my ancestor?" Miss Tinkerton asked.

"Yes. I'll read from the tablets."

"Come, Potter. You can finish that later." She dragged the professor from his plate and into the library, where Sam showed them all the 1620 tablets he had arranged in a neat row.

"These chapters were written by the Naugawump historian," he explained. "I'll begin with the part we are interested in." He started to read, looking up words in the clamshell dictionary when he had to.

Splashing Beaver brings Hobomock from another world. Hobomock escapes, steals sacred claw. Keewaytin angry.

"What's a Hobomock?" the professor asked.

"A sacrifice," Sam replied. He went on reading.

Great sadness. Keewaytin will eat Princess Minnetonka.

"Oh, how terrible!" Miss Tinkerton cried.

Sam read from another tablet. *Big canoe with white wings brings many strangers to land of Naugawumps.*

Now the mistress of the manor was really excited.

145

"The *Mayflower,* with ancestor John aboard!"

Hobomock and Tinkerton steal royal princess from sacred shrine.

"Oh, that brave John Tinkerton. He saved the Indian maiden's life. I told you he wasn't a bad boy."

"Wait," Sam said. "Listen to this."

Strangers from big canoe call Tinkerton kidnapper.

Her eyes widened in horror. "It says that? Does it say who was kidnapped?"

"Yes. The Hobomock who helped him rescue the princess."

That brought Miss Tinkerton close to tears. "I just can't believe it."

Sam couldn't believe it either. He knew it wasn't true.

"Easy now, Elvira," the professor said soothingly. "Are you sure, Sam? Let me see that chapter." He studied the tablet, checking it against the words in the dictionary. "I'm afraid that's what is written here, Elvira. Of course it could be wrong."

"It is wrong," Sam stated.

Miss Tinkerton smiled through her tears. "It is so kind of you to try to make me feel better but there's the evidence. I never should have opened up Queppish Hill. It just means more heartaches."

Sam banged the library table with his fist, rattling tablets and clamshells and startling his friends. "Yes, you should have. I know John Tinkerton didn't hurt me—him, I mean. The proof is here somewhere and I'm going to find it!"

He fell back into an armchair, wondering how.

146

22. THE OLD PARCHMENT

SINCE SAM had been up all night, Miss Tinkerton sent him to his room after breakfast to rest, while she and the professor went about their business. As he dozed off, the question kept bothering him: *Why did the Pilgrims accuse John of kidnapping me?*

When he awoke from his nap, he felt rested and a lot smarter. He took a bath in the big tub, put on clean clothes and hurried down to the library, knowing that the answer had to be somewhere in those tablets of Naugawump history.

Taking up the magnifying glass, he began translating again. That Indian historian sure knew a lot about the Pilgrims. When Diggins served lunch, Sam kept right on taking notes. By the end of the day, he had put together an amazing story. After dinner he made Professor Pittfall and Miss Tinkerton settle back in library chairs while he opened his notebook and read to them.

"It is the year sixteen twenty," he began. "John Tinkerton's friend is a sailor whom the Indians call Hobomock. He was stranded by an English ship the year before the Pilgrims landed and he's there on the beach when they arrive. He teaches them to fish and everybody likes him.

"One night the two young men leave Plymouth to hunt night crawlers. They are gone until daybreak. Tinkerton returns with the Indian princess but without his friend, Hobomock. When the Pilgrims ask where the sailor is, Tinkerton truthfully replies, 'I do not know.' When the sailor never returns, Tinkerton's hands and feet are put in the stocks. He will go on trial for kidnapping—maybe even murder."

Miss Tinkerton gasped, "Oh, my poor John!"

Sam continued. "The Pilgrims care for the princess but she soon becomes homesick. 'I must see my ill father, the Sachem Queppish,' she tells Tinkerton. 'Take me with you,' he begs her. She unlocks him from the stocks and they escape to the Naugawump village.

"Queppish lies there with many aching bones. He thanks Tinkerton for saving his daughter, Princess Minnetonka. The Naugawumps don't really want the huge lobster to eat her after all. That was the idea of Splashing Beaver, the medicine man, who has gone away."

Professor Pittfall frowned. "That name sounds familiar."

Sam quickly went on. "When Tinkerton asks where his sailor friend is, the Sachem replies, 'Splashing Beaver chased young Hobomock into another world.' "

The professor frowned even more. "Another world? Are you sure this isn't one of your jokes?"

148

"You can read the tablets yourself, Professor."

"Please go ahead, Sam," Miss Tinkerton requested. "Maybe we shall learn what happened to the fellow."

"Tinkerton asks Queppish, 'May I live with you? My people have falsely accused me of doing away with my friend.' The Naugawumps take him in. Tinkerton cures Queppish's illness by placing hot stones and steaming blankets on his joints. In gratitude, the Sachem grants him one wish. The young Englishman asks that Keewaytin eat no more people. The Sachem agrees to this and the Naugawumps cover the temple with dirt and sand, naming it Queppish Hill after their chief.

"Tinkerton is made an honorary member of the tribe. Then he hears bad news. His mother and father have been exiled from Plymouth as the parents of an escaped criminal. He goes to them and helps them build a home on a spot overlooking Tinkerton Sea, where the three of them take up life anew."

"That's where this manor house is right now!" Miss Tinkerton exclaimed.

Sam continued. "The Tinkerton family hopes for the return of the sailor, Hobomock, to prove that John did not kill him but he never appears. Splashing Beaver is not seen again either, although the Naugawumps say that his spirit visits Queppish Hill at night."

Sam put down his notebook. "That's as far as I went."

The Professor and Miss Tinkerton were silent for

a while. Finally the professor spoke. "I must say, my boy, you have done a remarkable job of translation. It's almost as though you had been there yourself."

"I've always been good at languages," Sam declared.

Miss Tinkerton was thoughtful. "It is quite an experience to hear at first hand about John. He found a cure for arthritis, I see."

"And the record shows that he didn't harm anyone," Sam pointed out.

She smiled sadly. "To us maybe, but it is hardly enough to end the Tinkerton Curse."

"Why not, Elvira?" the professor asked.

"The townspeople of Plymouth would never accept the word of some unnamed Naugawump historian. The story will look like a put-up job to anyone but us, especially because I hired you. We need real proof and there doesn't seem to be any."

Sam had to grit his teeth to keep from saying, *I am the proof. I was there and I am here. I am alive.* Just another practical joke, they would say, and they wouldn't think it was funny. So he didn't open his mouth. Instead, he racked his brains for another way to show that the Pilgrims had made a big mistake in banishing the Tinkertons.

"You know what, Miss Tinkerton?" he said. "We ought to look at that paper again, the one your father told you about."

"We have looked at it already, Sam. I showed it to you."

"I mean, we ought to read what it says. It might give us a clue or something."

She shook her head. "I don't think it can be opened. It's much too flimsy. It would just fall to pieces."

The professor spoke up. "That's nothing to worry about, Elvira. I have some vellum mulsifier that will soften the parchment without hurting it. I use it all the time on Egyptian papyrus."

"Well, if you think it might do some good—"

She took the old document from the safe and the professor brought in a bottle of vellum mulsifier from the safari wagon. Then they gathered around the kitchen sink. After pouring some of the chemical into a baking dish, Pittfall placed the parchment in it and let it soak, gently turning it over until it became limp. After that he carefully unrolled it, using a wooden spoon and his fingers. When it was flat, he lifted it out of the dish and laid it on a kitchen towel to soak up the chemical. Eagerly they bent over the old brown parchment to read the faded writing.

Peering through his magnifying glass, the professor said, "It's in an old English. Take this down."

Sam grabbed the notebook.

Whereas, in the year sixteen hundred twenty, we, the loyal subjects of His Grace, James the First, having gathered for the preservation, security and peace of the New World, and having found the family Tinkerton guilty of disobedience to the just laws of our Colony, do hereby banish said family from Plymouth environs now and forevermore.

152

To wit: John, son of Squire Tinkerton, is under suspicion of the most foul deed of murder, having caused to be lost, kidnapped, and mayhap done away with, the person known as the sailor, one Samuel Christopher Churchill of parts unknown. . . .

"What?"

Their cries echoed off the walls of the big kitchen. The professor and Miss Tinkerton stared in astonishment at Sam, who was just as amazed as they were. His name was in the document, written more than three hundred and fifty years ago.

"Samuel!" Miss Tinkerton said when she recovered from her surprise. "This could have been the mysterious ancestor of yours that your mother spoke about. He's the same sailor who—well, I can hardly believe it. Imagine that!"

Professor Pittfall bent over the parchment again. "Yes, there's no question about it." He straightened up. "By the way, Sam, what is your middle name?"

"Christopher, the same as my father's. It's been in the family for a long time, they tell me."

"What a coincidence," Miss Tinkerton murmured.

"It's more than that," Sam said excitedly as he realized what it meant. "Don't you see? Now everyone will know that John Tinkerton did not do away with the sailor, Samuel Christopher Churchill. Because if Churchill had been murdered, he couldn't have grown up, had children, passed down his name, and I would not exist. I am his direct descendant.

"This ends the Curse of the Tinkertons once and for all!"

AFTERWORD

AFTER PROFESSOR PITTFALL and Sam finished collecting and recording the objects taken from Queppish Hill, they put them all back where they had found them. Then the old temple was opened to the public and named the John Tinkerton Memorial Museum. Because it was one of the best collections of Naugawump artifacts, visitors came to it from far and wide. The tablets and the famous clamshell dictionary made it possible to learn more about the Naugawumps than had ever been known before.

When Elvira Tinkerton made her first visit to Plymouth, she went straight to the Office of the Mayor to demand that the order of exile be canceled. She took Sam with her to prove that his ancestor could not have been murdered by John Tinkerton in 1620. The mayor greeted her warmly and reported that no record of the exile document could be found in the files. Also he said that no one he had talked to in Plymouth could remember why the Tinkertons had stayed away from town for so long. The Town Council invited her to be a judge at the next Pilgrim Day parade.

One day Professor Potter B. Pittfall packed all his belongings into Lulu and went on his way. The Maharajah of Downpour had invited him to spend the rest of the season in his palace in the cool mountains of northern India. There the two old friends would go by hang glider to the hidden Kush Valley to search for the lost marbles of Alexander the Great.

When Sam boarded the bus to go back home, Miss Tinkerton kissed him good-bye and invited him to come for a visit the following summer. He promised to do that.

When he arrived home, his mother prepared a New England clambake as a special treat. He enjoyed it. After he finished it, he took a lobster claw from the pot, polished it and hung it on his bedpost. Next year, he decided, when he returned to Plymouth, he was going to carry the claw with him on a canoe trip through the Tunnel to Yesterday— just to see what might happen.

A FEW WORDS FROM
THE CLAMSHELL DICTIONARY
NAUGAWUMP-ENGLISH

AGWONK, birthplace; home.

AHQUAY, hello; good day.

GOOGLUSH, fool; stupid.

GOOMBA, fast; hurry.

GUTCH, moon.

HUA, full; big.

KEESUQUIT, prayer.

KEESWUSH, season; time.

KOTCHANUNK, brown.

KTAMONK, health; goodness.

KUHTAH, grateful; thanks.

KUKKETAFF, wealth; plenty.

KUTTENAN, roof; ceiling.

MATTERLAWAWA, beans.

MICHEENEE, insect.

MUNATCH, luck; fortune.

NAMASSACK, fish; seafood.

NEESHUN, listen; pay attention.

NEETCHY, come; follow.

NUMKONK, sacred claw.

NUMMANUNK, blue.

NUMMET, enter; arrive.

OUGANIT, forever; always.

PEYAUM, perfect; wise.

PQTCHX, pqtchx.

POCKATUNK, lobster.

QUAY, good; happy.

QUITTIANIT, necessary; helpful.

SAKOPAGUNKUM, abracadabra.

SHO-SHO, farewell.

SONGASH, sun; sunshine.

SQUANAMOCK, weeds.

SUQUEESHY, eel.

SUTKOKISH, remove; take away.

TAMOOK, hole; opening.

UTCH, bring; carry.

WAPPINUNK, yellow.

WEEBY, eye.

YUKKEE, out; over.

NOTE

WHEN the Pilgrims landed in 1620, the Indians in southeastern Massachusetts belonged to the Wampanoag tribe. The language they spoke has been forgotten but many of the words have been written down, and many names, such as Queppish, still survive. The Naugawump words in this book are loosely based on them.